ROSCOMMON
FOLK
TALES

CW00550676

ROSCOMMON
FOLK TALES

PAT WATSON

ILLUSTRATED BY
PATRICIA WATSON

The
History
Press
Ireland

First published 2013, reprinted 2016

The History Press Ireland
50 City Quay
Dublin 2
Ireland
www.thehistorypress.ie

The History Press Ireland is a member of Publishing Ireland,
the Irish book publishers' association.

British Library Cataloguing in Publication Data.
A catalogue record for this book is available from the British Library.

ISBN 978 1 84588 784 1

Typesetting and origination by The History Press
Printed and bound by TJ International Ltd.

CONTENTS

ACKNOWLEDGEMENTS

I would like to thank the following for their help with this book: Evelyn Watson; Mattie Ward; Gearoid O'Brien; Richard Finan; Tom Tighe; Maura Quigley; Tim O'Connell; Fred Carney; Patrica Watson; Anthony Tuohy; Don Feeley; Michael Martin; Aidan Kelleher; Fr Michael Kelly; Fr Ciaran Whitney; Frank Tivnan; John Kerrigan; and Sean Byrne.

1

THE VISIONARY

Even before her birth Ashling was different. She kicked so hard at night that she woke both her parents. The strange thing was that whenever she woke them it was always for some reason – the cow was calving, Granny had fainted, the hens were being attacked by the fox or the neighbour's house was on fire – and in all these cases disasters were averted. So, when Ashling finally arrived in this world with a peculiar birthmark the shape of an Irish wolfhound on her shoulder it was taken as a sign that she was destined for greatness or disaster. Indeed, the wise old woman who brought her into the world said she was privileged to birth such a treasure before she died.

'I have been waiting for this for all of fifty years and isn't it wonderful that I lived to see it. Our Earth God has been kind to me. Indeed, this may be the child who will one day, in the very distant future, inspire a descendant to capture the mystery, magic, lore and history of this era and area' she said. 'Her mother, Ina, was one of the tree people who were descended from the magical Tuatha Dé Danann.'

Various early peoples are said to have come to Ireland by sea but the magical Tuatha Dé Danann came on the wind from Tír na nÓg (The Land of Youth). They it was who created the soul of the Irish and who imbued all who came before or after with the Irish Spirit. This included a natural ability in music, speech, poetry, sport, laughter and merriment and a little portion of magic that is known as 'craic'. They were also hot-tempered, strong, brave, daring and often rash. However, even if they lost in battle to strangers, which they usually did, within a few generations the spirit of the Tuatha Dé Danann would have seeped into the blood and mind of the strangers. Thereafter the magic never left them no matter how far they wandered or how great their number. Tír na nÓg was not a real place but a state of mind.

She grew up in the shadow of the great Fort of Cruachán and was a very bright child. By the time she was six she could milk a goat or catch and kill a hare or even grab passing crows or seagulls. Needless to say this made her family well fed with meat and milk.

There were no schools then and children learned from their mothers, fathers, siblings and neighbours. From an early age, however, Ashling saw things that others could not see. She would say she saw men in red coats riding horses on the road. Of course there were no roads there at that time and certainly no men in red coats. Some said she was a little queer, others said she was magically gifted with seeing the past or the future. She was always seeing people but she never knew any of them. Eventually word of her visions travelled to Rickpat, the king of the fort.

King Rickpat decided that she might be very useful to him so he sent his best man riding a horse, to collect her. She did not like the man on the horse and said she would not go with him. Her mother and father did not want her to go but they depended on the king to protect them against the raiders that sometimes came from the north. But when they ordered her to go she refused point blank. As she was only a little girl the horseman just picked her up under his arm and galloped away. She did not cry out but only said, 'When he dies I will have to walk home.'

Her mother and the neighbours listened well but the horseman just laughed as he trotted away. Just as they came in sight of the fort a fox jumped out in front of them and though the rider nearly kept control, the horse veered under a low-hanging branch. The rider hit his head and fell dead on the ground. The child dropped

safely to the ground, the horse galloped away, and Ashling walked all the way home.

When King Rickpat heard what happened he became even more determined to have this unique child in his fort, where he could use her visions and magic to his advantage. However, he could not afford to lose any more men, and anyhow he had no men brave enough to tackle this magic child. He asked his wife for ideas to capture this treasure but she was not enthusiastic, as she believed that magic was dangerous and would bring no good.

'Beware,' she said, 'she may come to control you and yours.' Rickpat was sure that the gods sent this child for his benefit. Finally, he formed a plan in his own mind. He would offer the parents, Num and Ina, a house and position within the fort and then he would be near the little one and he could hear her himself.

Shortly before this, the king had skirted the great bog of Trim and captured extensive lands stretching all the way to the great river, Shannon. He had forced the people there to pay tribute of cattle, sheep and poultry, but it was a long way around the bog and it took nearly all his men coming and going to keep the people there subdued. What he needed was a short way across the soft shivering bog. It was so soft and marshy that only hares could traverse it on their own well-used paths. A wise druid had told him that in other parts, kings had found a way of making roads on the bogs with wattles but when he and his men tried it, all they achieved was getting very wet and dirty.

He could kill two birds with just one stone.

Next time he called to the house of Ashling himself. Her parents were too much in awe of the king to say anything, so he said to Ashling, 'And how is my little girl today?'

'I'm fine thank you,' she said, 'but I am not your little girl; I belong to my Mammy and Daddy.'

'But I am the king,' he said.

'I know who you are and I know who I am,' she replied.

'Are you not afraid of me?' he asked.

'Why? Are you a bad man?'

'No! No! No! I am not a bad man. Actually I've come to offer your father a great opportunity, in fact the opportunity of a lifetime. I want all of you to come to live within the fort. Then I want your father, Num, to take twenty men and try to make a road across the bog of Trim.' The parents both knew that others had failed at this task and they suspected that it was only a ruse to get the child into the fort. The king noticed the hesitation and immediately said, 'You will have your own house and the use of a few acres outside the fort, within the enclosure, and you can come and go as you please. Ina and the child will have ladies and their children for company. Sure, we'll all be one big happy family. Think about it for a bit while I go see your goats,' he said.

'What do you think?' said Num, after the king left.

'Do we have much choice?' asked Ina who was a bit afraid but was also anxious to get into the fort and be upwardly mobile.

'How am I going to do any better at road making than the others who tried?' said Num.

'I will help,' said Ashling.

'And how will a little fairy like you help?' asked Num as he picked her up so they could rub noses.

'You will see.'

When the king came back they agreed to his terms and within a few days they were in comfortable quarters in the fort, while their goats, hens, ducks, geese, were safely in the little farmyard that came with the few acres. Num would get time off from overseeing road building to sow the corn.

On arrival at the fort, Ashling was immediately surrounded by six giant Irish wolfhounds that were used for hunting deer. They towered over her and licked her face. When she waved a tiny warning finger at them and ordered them to have manners they obeyed immediately. Their names were Mussy, Blackie, Nick, Butch, Hendrix and Spot. The king's seven-year-old son Hau was most impressed as he was afraid of the dogs, and thenceforth all eight of them were dedicated playmates.

Work started on the road the next day. It was springtime and there was great excitement on the edge of the bog. Skylarks, pilibins, storks, curlews, hen harriers, snipes, water hens and others were busy with boisterous mating and nesting, with the occasional

Irish Wolfhound

hungry eagle watching from far above. From the edge of the great oak forest the natural hazel covered the ground down to the marsh where they were joined by the sallies, birch, sedge grass and finally heather. A gravel road could be made through the first hundred yards as the upland slowly slanted downward beneath the marsh.

The king decreed that the road over the bog should be the width of one big man lying crosswise with his hands stretched above his head, about seven feet. First they extracted the gravel and stones from Cairn Hill. This took six weeks as the further they went the higher the road had to be to compensate for the falling ground. In the end, the road was five feet high but was only level with the adjoining bog. Now was the moment of truth. What would happen when they went on to the bog? The last failure stood as a reminder just a few yards away.

During those weeks, Ashling, Hau and the wolfhounds were gathering little sally rods to make their own road. The rods that they broke off were only as thick as her little finger. Even so the first break was never complete and they had to twist them for a complete break. When they had a lot of sticks – an unknown number, as they could not count – she put half of them lengthwise and the other half crosswise. All eight now walked across the sticks but they rolled apart. Then she had a great idea: she would weave them together.

When this was done, the sticks supported the eight, even across very soft ground where the muck had been up to their ankles. Some muck came up and through, but the rods held together. When her father saw this he knew his problems were solved.

'You never let me down,' he said as he picked her up to rub noses.

'Hau helped too,' she said. Hau's face reddened, as he knew he had only looked on but he was very pleased by the compliment bestowed by the little vision.

Num and his men pulled a great lot of heather first and placed it on the bog. Then they put wattles thicker than a man's wrist

crosswise and lengthwise enmeshed together and put them on top
of the heather. Then they brought scraws from the upland and put
them on the top. When they walked on to the road it shivered
a little but held firm. When one of the cows was led on to the
contraption it shivered and dipped a little more but did not break
and held fast even as several cows were walked and circled about
on it. The king and everybody were delighted. The problem was
solved; they could make their road. Better still, the king had the
little magician within his reach!

The king and his men went hunting deer every few days with
the six wolfhounds in the forest Futch that was called after the
stammering Fut, the king of the underworld. The Tuatha Dé
Danann had locked Fut under a great boulder and by a magic web
in Oweynagat, the Cave of Cats, which was deep in the woods.

One day, Ashling said to Hau, 'Why don't you and I go hunting
with the hounds, we might catch hares or even deer?'

'What if we meet wolves?'

'The barking of the hounds will keep the wolves away till darkness.'

'No, we cannot go into the woods because we might meet a
bear, what would we do then?'

Ashling said no more, but a few days later she asked again, 'Why can't we go?'

'I told you,' Hau said, 'we might meet a bear.'

'And we might not.'

'But if we did?'

'The hounds will mind us,' she replied.

'What if we get lost?'

'We won't; we can watch the sunlight through the trees.'

Hau thought about this. She had been right about a lot of things, was she right now?' Should he take the chance? He did not want to look weak.

'Please,' she said, with a wistful smile and a sparkle in her deep blue eyes, pushing back her mop of auburn hair. That did it. They would go but nobody must know.

They set off, and after a little while they would look back, carry on for a bit, look back, then another little bit before they got to the woods and could no longer be seen. Very soon the dogs picked up a scent and away they went at great speed. The children followed as best they could, shouting at the dogs to slow down, but soon enough the dogs were in the ever-increasing distance. Their barking grew faint and faded away altogether. The children stopped for they could no longer tell which way the dogs had gone. They looked at each other and each little worried face scared the other.

'Are we lost?' said Ashling, with a trembling lip. Hau remembered what she had said about seeing the sun through the trees. He looked up but it seemed the day had darkened and there was no sign of the sun. The Sun God had gone to sleep. They had forgotten to pray to him this morning. He must be angry. Hau decided he would not blame Ashling, for she was too beautiful. He would act like a man even if he did not feel like one. So he put his arm round her shoulder and said it will be all right, the dogs would come back and even if they didn't, they would still find their way home.

They walked and walked for a long time but did not reach the edge of the woods nor could they hear any but woodland sounds. Whenever they disturbed a woodcock and it fluttered up before them, they were frightened. They saw a huge tree with a mighty hole at ground level, and inside the hole was a sort of lair as if for a mighty hare.

They took no further notice but continued on their way home. They were growing tired and thirsty but it was not far now. Then they came to the tree with the mighty hole again. They were lost and just walking in circles. Each little face looked at each other. Tears were very near, and just then the first clatter of thunder rolled up the sky far above and the clouds burst, the rain hammering on the canopy above. Within seconds huge blobs of water would roll off the leaves and drench them. Shaking with fright, they shrieked loudly before they took shelter in the comfy tree.

When the queen and Ina heard the thunder, both ran out to get the children. They were gone! The dogs were gone! Consternation broke out. They must have gone to the woods. Would the dogs protect them and bring them home safely? Little did they know that the children were sheltering alone in the bear's den a mile west of the fort.

When the bear heard the thunder he was in a clearing in the wood raiding bees' nests a mile north of his den. He decided to head for home.

When the hounds heard the thunder they had just slain a deer and were waiting for their masters to catch up and carry home the prey. They were two miles west of the children. Then Butch, the biggest and fiercest, heard the distant shriek. He eyed Mussy and Spot to stay while he and the other four bounded away.

When Num and his men heard the thunder they immediately headed home, as flat ground was dangerous in lightning and besides, they were not dressed for heavy rain.

When the king heard the thunder he was outside repairing the palisade that surrounded the little fields around the fort, and he too headed home.

Meanwhile, the mothers of the children had raised such a wail that several men with spears, slings, arrows, sticks and stones had gathered. The king led them to the forest but they were not sure which way to go.

The bear was making slow, steady progress, as he did not like getting wet.

Butch and the other three dogs were barking loudly as they headed in the direction of the children. Luckily, the men coming in the opposite direction heard them and headed to meet them. The bear arrived at the tree first, but he was distracted by the lightning-fast howling dogs. When he turned to face them they quickly spread out all around him with Butch and Blackie keeping between him and the den. Wolfhounds are brave, fierce and fast but are no match for a bear. Only for the cries of the children they would have given him a wide berth. The bear, however, was not prepared to give up and headed straight for the tree. With a great bound Butch sprung up on his back and bit deep into the thick

skin on the back of his neck. The bear stopped, reached back with his two paws and pulled the dog out over his head and began to tear poor Butch apart. The dog managed a dying lunge and bit a huge lump off the top of the bear's nose. He died with the bear's nose in his teeth.

Just then, the men arrived and began to pelt the bear with all the force of their weaponry and voices. Being mesmerised by the ferocity and huge numbers of his attackers the bear headed west and was chased for many miles into new territory, and he was never seen again.

Meanwhile, the women and the boys arrived and, after much hugging, took home the children. The men recovered the deer on their way back and a great feast was had by all.

Hau was struck dumb, but Ashling was inconsolable at the ferocity of the fight and, above all, at the loss of her beloved Butch. Ina held her close for a long time but finally gave her a little mead, lulling her into a fitful sleep.

As she slept, Ina watched over her and was surprised when a smile appeared on her pale little face.

Ashling heard the two Leprechauns at the same time as she saw them. They were talking to each other. She never knew before that Leprechauns spoke in Limericks only.

The first one said:

There was a great wolfhound called Butch,
Who loved his young mistress too much.
For Ashling and Crown,
He laid his life down.
Now he'll be the great Legend of Futch.

The second one said:

Great Butch was the bravest hound ever,
Would he flee from the big bear? No, never,
Though he pulled him apart,
And tore out his heart,
He managed the bear's nose to sever.

That was when her mother saw her smile, and little Ashling never
mourned Butch again.

2

WARS, WEDDINGS
AND PREDICTIONS

Over the following years, Ashling and Hau became inseparable. The wolfhound Nick had three pups; the biggest was called Butch, the other two were Bailey and Sparkey. The children and the dogs became so good at hunting that soon everybody was eating deer at least once a week.

When Ashling was just thirteen years old, word reached the King Rickpat and all the Connaught men, that the King of Leigin had developed bows and arrows and that his men could kill with the new contraption at twenty paces. The Connaught men were fierce spear fighters and they had arrows but they could only fire at ten paces and were not very accurate, while spears are only good at two paces unless they were thrown and when the enemy collected them, they could throw them back.

Connaught had a big problem as the men of Leigin were marching to cross the Shannon at Athlone. The kingdoms of Monksland, Kiltoom and Cam called on King Rickpat for help: 'If you save us from this enemy, we will be subject to you thereafter and we will pay you tribute every harvest.'

King Rickpat sent for Ashling.

'Have you any idea how we can defend ourselves against those new weapons that the Leigin men have?'

Ashling closed her eyes and after a while she said, 'Give me a little while to think.'

When she closed her eyes a thought occurred to her. She felt that what was happening should be recorded for posterity and she was obliged to do it. She opened her eyes and looked about. The landscape was totally different – the forests were gone, and the timber fence that surrounded the fort and the little fields was gone without trace. The bog and lake had dried out and was green and luscious; there was no sign of the Forest of Futch. She saw the extent of a realm much larger than Cruachán. It covered an area that would one day be called Roscommon. It will be called after the Christian St Coman, who will build a monastery beside a wood. It will be the first county in Ireland when a future king, Phelim O'Conor, changed the name to County Roscommon. It will be divided into areas called parishes. She drew out their shapes in the dust with her finger. They extended from the Shannon to the Suck for a very long way. She instinctively knew the names of those parishes. Then it hit her. She was seeing things Melina hence. If she was going to inspire somebody from that time she would need to use the place names that she saw or heard in her mind.

The visions had a narrow focus on one place only. Sometimes they moved sideways to giver a wider view but other times they stayed in the same place but moved through time. This made them hard to understand and a vision is always hard to turn into words especially if times are very different.

The king returned. 'Well,' he said, 'any ideas about defending Connaught?'

'Can you not hold them at the river at Athlone?' Ashling asked.

'No, because they come in boats and they will be able to shoot down our men from the boats at twenty paces while we will only be able to defend at two feet. We have only a limited number of spears.'

Ashling closed her eyes again and concentrated. 'All of the land west of Athlone is swampy bog except the narrow Esker that runs down to and through the Shannon. Build a timber palisade of strong uprights, one and a half man high across the esker, with half man high earth walkway on our side. Our men can duck the arrows and

spear the enemy when they come close. Then build a bog roadway
just two paces wide, going south in the soft ground for a thousand
paces. Build two other roads ten paces longer just a half a pace from
the middle road. Cover all three roads with heather but have the
heather much deeper and standing erect on the outer roads. Divide
your men into four ways. Put one lot looking over the palisade, two
larger numbers hiding in the heather on the two outer roads. The
last lot, who will have to be the bravest and will face the enemy on
the riverbank, they will duck the first lot of arrows as best they can
and then turn and run down the middle road. When the Leigin
men see the cowards run they will not bother to reload the bows but
will rush ashore and follow our men along the bog road. When they
are spread out along the middle road our men will rise out of the
heather on either side and stab them. When any that are not killed
in the first surprise attack try to fight back, they will sink in the half
paces between the roads. If any try to run back our men from the
palisades will cut off their retreat.'

This was done over the next few days and the men of Monksland,
Kiltoom and Cam marvelled at being able to traverse the swamp.
When the Leigin men saw the apparently cowardly Connaught
men retreat, they quickly paddled their boats ashore and bounded
after the fleeing sissies just as Ashling had foretold. Just as the last
of them started on the bog road the hidden Connaught men rose
up and slew them.

≈❀≈

The following year, just after the harvest, a plea came from the
kingdom of Boyle for help defending against a mighty army from
Ulla that was marching south and would come east of the mountains. At that time, the kingdom of Boyle stretched around the
mountains to Keadue, Arigna and Ballyfarnon. The Boyle king
promised total allegiance to Cruachán and Rickpat if they saved
him and his people. All the Connaught kingdoms knew that they
could not match the mighty men of Ulla.

Rickpat went to Ashling.

'What can we do?' he asked.

Ashling once again closed her eyes and thought for a while, then she said, 'Send emissaries to talk terms with the Ulla king. Keep them talking on the high barren ground until the full moon twenty days hence. Then agree to whatever terms demanded with the proviso that the emissaries return a day ahead of the army to tell the Connaught to lay down arms.'

At first the king was not convinced but when he remembered Athlone he slowly nodded agreement. The Boyle people were very doubtful but they too had heard of Athlone and anyhow sooner or later they would have to settle for complete surrender. They did as they were told.

Sure enough, the emissaries met the Ulla's on the high ground where they started to negotiate. Their first offer was refused outright. They sent a runner back to Boyle, and he came back the next day with a much better offer. The king of Ulla felt he had the upper hand and refused that offer too. The runner ran again and returned the next day with a better offer that was once again refused. This happened every day until the full moon, when complete surrender and subjugation was agreed. The only thing the emissaries asked for was for one day to gather up all their men in case any might rebel. The Ulla's agreed and let them go.

That evening the wind blew down from the north and it began to snow. As it was not very late in the year, the army, while they were a bit uncomfortable felt it would be gone by morning. It wasn't. The next morning, the snow was heavier, the wind stronger and the cold unbearable. Worse still, the drifts were so huge that they were completely grounded. If this lasted long they would die of cold and hunger in this barren place. It did and they did. The Connaught men were saved. The next day Ashling said, 'The place where the Ulla men died will be a lucky place of future battles associated with the magical Lough Cé close by.'

Soon after, when Ashling was just fifteen and Hau sixteen, King Rickpat took the coughing and in spite of every effort of the druids he passed away within the week. There was a great ceremonial funeral and he was cremated within sight of Cruachán and his ashes brought and buried near Carnfree.

As Hau was now to be crowned king, he asked Ashling to marry him, she accepted and they were crowned king and queen together. The crowning took place standing on the crowning stone on the hill of Carnfree. Everybody agreed that they were the most handsome and suitable couple ever to marry. They were blissfully happy. Why, they had grown up together nearly as one and had waited patiently for this glorious day. Their happiness knew no bounds, ecstasy beyond words.

They both knew that Roscommon, as it was now called, would always be the bulwark that would protect Connaught from attacks of every sort.

Ashling told Hau that a great kingdom was developing in the east that would be called Tara and, at that moment, there was a very clever family of druids who were drawing up plans to build a mighty monument to be aligned with the sun and that will last forever. 'They could not do this,' she said, 'if my people the Tuatha Dé Danann had not confined Fut in Oweynagat, the Cave of Cats. Tara will be the home of many High Kings and our Realm will be known as the Tara of the West. For here will live the Kings of Connaught and indeed many High Kings of Ireland.'

3

THE LAST BIT OF THE REALM

A rider, Sean, came from the south in great haste to the fort. 'The raiders from Mua, who came from the southwest, have overrun the two Drum forts and the Drum people have fled north to the oak forest of Cam. They are making a stand there and they need help.' This was the first problem for the new young king. After all, he was only sixteen, and so he turned to his fifteen-year-old wife, Ashling.

'What will you do for us for our trouble?' she asked softly.

'Our great King Han and all his family were killed and now we are leaderless. We heard how you dealt with the Ullas and Leigins. Will you become our king and all our lands will be yours?'

'Who are you?' asked the king.

'My seven brothers and I are nephews of the dead king and all the people have elected us to ask for your protection. Two of my brothers are with the people in Cam forest. The other four rode with me. One is resting five miles back waiting my return. The other is ten miles back, the third twenty miles back, the fourth thirty miles and the youngest a further ten miles awaiting your decision. As I had the fastest horse, I came all the way as the others stopped by the wayside to rest. When I relate your decision they will relay it back while I rest my horse. We can have your reply back to Cam by morning.'

'After you're fed, go back and tell your people that we are coming with thousands of men and with the same magic that wiped out the men from Ulla and Leigin. Make sure to send a spy to inform the Mua army of the plan.'

'But then, they will be prepared and will be all the harder to defeat.'

'I think they will run for their lives if they have any sense,' said the king. 'And we will march tomorrow.'

Sean was so delighted that he gulped down his food and drink and rode back to meet his brother.

Ashling turned to her new husband in a sort of daze and said, 'One day in the distant future, there are many stories about Roscommon and how it came to be and our descendants will record them together with the happenings of our times.'

He gently kissed her and brought her back to reality and his warm embrace.

The relay team were back in Cam shortly after daybreak. When the spy informed the Mua army of their coming doom they did just as the king said and fled back across the river Suck from whence they had come.

4

LOUGH CÉ

Originally, the Tuatha Dé Danann had three tribes, the Shea, the Bhea and the Nuadha, whose king had a silver arm and who was known as Nuadha of the Silver Arm.

All three tribes had been at war for generations and they had worked so much magic, moving mountains and lakes and disappearing hills and hollows, that it was no longer possible to live on their land of Tír na nÓg – all the water there had flowed down a great hole that the Nuadha had made to drown the other two tribes. However, the God of Water got angry with the Nuadha and banished them down the hole and decreed that they could never climb out.

Now that the land of Tír na nÓg had no water, the Shea and the Bhea came on the wind to Ireland. They landed on the south end of the Curlew Mountains and looked about them. The young king, whose name was Amor, led the Bhea, and his chief druid was Ola. The Shea were led by the beautiful Queen Oram, and her top druid was Oli. Because the two tribes had been at war for a long time, the druids of both tribes held a meeting between them and decided that the King of Bhea was to marry the Queen of Shea, to stop the wars. They colluded to produce the most powerful love potions, and they were very powerful love potions as they were great druids with wonderful magic. They made one male and one female potion. Now the problem was how to get both parties to take their potion at the same time and to get them to meet each other and no one else before the potions wore out.

The Bhea had moved to the Ballyfarnon area while the Shea were in the Boyle region. At that time, there was no lake where Lough Cé is now, only a bubbling, sparkling spring well. The druids decided to try to get the king and queen to meet at a huge high rock that towered above the sparkling spring well. They decided that they would convince Amor to climb one side of the rock and at the same time get Oram to sing sweetly on the other side. This had to happen late on the night of a full moon for the potions to work.

Now, Ola and Oli had made a terrible mistake and mixed up the two potions, each having the wrong one. Ola brought Amor to the north side of the rock and advised him to climb to the top with him. Ola then produced the potion and told Amor that he had to be alone on this rock, facing the full moon when he drank it. Then he was to raise his arms to the moon and ask to be accepted in this new land. Ola then slipped away down the rock and hid behind a bush. Amor did as he was instructed for he trusted Ola and his magic. The plan was that while Omar was addressing the moon he would hear the sweet singing and go to investigate. When he would see the beautiful Oram he would immediately fall for her.

Just about the time that Ola was instructing Omar, Oli and Oram arrived at the south side of the rock. Oli then advised Oram to wait till he had gone, then drink the potion and sing sweetly to the moon and she and her tribe would be accepted in this new land. She drank the concoction that was meant for a man and immediately felt manly, strong, daring and protective. Instead of singing sweetly she bounded up the rock face.

After Omer had drunk the female potion, instead of conversing with the moon, he looked about him and took fright at his plight on the top of a dangerously high rock. So he lay down, leaned on one elbow, held a jutting rock tight with the other hand and whimpered sadly. About this time Oram arrived at the summit and started to console Omer.

Far below, both watching Ola and Oli realized their mistake at the same time. They rushed around the rock to meet each other. At first they started to argue, each blaming the other for the mistake but as they looked up and saw the calamity unfolding above they decided not to just stand there, but do something. They thought that when the love potions wore off that both Monarchs would be embarrassed and angry with themselves, their silly behaviour, their position, but above all with the two druids. Men had died for smaller errors.

Unknown to them all, Cé, the druid of Nuadha, had piggy-backed on the tail of the wind that carried the two tribes to Ireland. Cé had watched the entire proceedings from behind a bush that grew on a high rocky outcrop a distance east of the rock that the royal couple were on. He was waiting and watching for a chance to avenge the banishment of his King Nuadha of the Silver Arm down the hole.

We need another plan, they said, but what? Then Ola said, 'The only thing that will make them forget their present silly behaviour after the potions wane is a terrible fright. Remember how terrified they both were when the Nuadha were threatening to throw them down the water hole?'

'I have it,' said Oli. 'We will make the well overflow at great speed and turn this whole area into a lake and when they awake from their stupor they will be stranded on the rock and we will be watching from the high ground of the mountain foothills in the west.' They pooled all their power, made great incantations, did many magic dances, shimmied about each other, and called sincerely on all the Gods, especially the God of Water. That did the trick. Their prayers were answered and the well began to overflow. Ola and Oli ran for higher ground.

When Cé saw what was happening he was delighted and he decided that he would be the one to rescue the royal pair when the flood receded. He would have Ola and Oli killed or banished. Then he would start a fight between Oram and Omer that might yet lead to the rescue of his tribe from their plight down the hole. However, Cé had underestimated the power of the flood and very soon the waters lapped about his feet, his knees, his head and then completely over his hideout. He was pulled down by the waters and was the first one to be drowned in the new lake. Before his last gasp he asked just one final favour from the Water God. Would he put a curse on the royal couple on the rock or on a pair of their descendants? The Water God reluctantly agreed to the latter and Cé gulped a lungful of water and drowned. The lake was named after him when they found his body.

Meanwhile, unaware of Cé's presence, Ola and Oli ran for their lives and only barely made the high ground in front of the expanding waters. When they looked back from their high perch, the sun was just coming up the far side of the most beautiful lake they had ever seen. There were several beautiful islands scattered about and the rock was just peeping in the middle of the lake, with the two Monarchs clinging in terror to the only little shrub there and to each other. Luckily for all the lake stopped expanding at this point.

At first, gasping in wonder and awe, the two druids prostrated themselves to thank all the gods they had prayed to, especially the God of Water. Then, being our druids, they saw the funny side of things and rolled about laughing merrily. Then reality dawned. How were they going to rescue the clinging pair? And what would the mood be when they did so? Would it be a matter of life or death? Whose life? Whose death?

They put on their thinking caps again. There were a couple of rotting trunks from trees that had been blown down by storms a long time ago. If they could mesh those together with light hazel wattles that were abundant about them, they might have a floatable raft. They worked feverishly, and after an hour they launched the contraption. It actually floated. Gingerly they climbed aboard. They paddled slowly with branches. They were terrified. Would they be the first to be drowned in the new lake? Would their magic be their undoing? Would the Gods stay benevolent? As some progress was made, their courage increased. Over the next hour they were so busy paddling, steering and steadying their craft that they never once checked out the pair on the rock. When they finally reached their destination the two monarchs scarcely noticed them as they held hands, gazed into each other's eyes and talked the talk of lovers. They would be the first of many loving couples, happy, magic and tragic to be associated with this scenic rock in Roscommon's most beautiful lake.

The druid's magic ruse had succeeded in a totally unexpected way. The tribes were united and happy. The people were united and happy. The Tuatha Dé Danann were united and happy, the druids were united and happy but above all the young couple were united and happy ever after. They and their descendants would live in Roscommon and Ireland, and sooner or later would imbue everyone else in Roscommon and Ireland and the Irish Diaspora throughout the world with their merry, musical, mystical, magical, poetic and playful spirit.

5

THE BATTLE ABOVE
LOUGH CÉ

The area above Lough Cé, known as the Curlew Pass, was always known as the lucky ground, as it was said that the Roscommon men had a great victory there in ancient times.

When an Englishman called Clifford came to Athlone Castle in the sixteenth century he did not realise as he crossed the Shannon that he was coming into the territory of the magic people. The little people visited him in his dreams. They showed him his headless body being carried, prayed over and finally buried by shrouded holy monks. When he mentioned this to some of his friends they asked if he has over indulged in poteen (illicit Irish whiskey).

A few days later, Clifford led a fine English army of horse and foot soldiers from Athlone, through Roscommon, Tulsk and Boyle, on their way to meet O'Connor conspirators in Coolooney Castle, who were under siege there by the Irish O'Donnell. However, O'Donnell had anticipated their coming and asked the Roscommon troops, led by Brian Oge O'Rourke and Conar MacDermott, for help. They sent false information to Clifford that the Curlew Pass was deserted and not defended by the Irish. Going on this information, Clifford did not rest at Boyle but continued to march on to the pass. He was also completely unaware of the Curlew magic that was used before and would be used again to win battles here. He was also unaware that this magic works better in the fall of the year. This time the Irish were well prepared and did not have to wait for the snow.

At the pass, the Irish were lying in wait and in ninety minutes routed the English, killed 500 and chased the rest back to Boyle Abbey. Clifford was killed and his severed head handed to O'Donnell. He brought the head back to Coolooney Castle to intimidate its defenders. O'Connor was indeed intimidated, so much so, that he surrendered and joined O'Donnell's army. This victory gave heart to many Irish to desert the English army and join the Irish freedom fighters. The McDermott's brought Clifford's body to the monastery in Lough Cé where the monks gave it a Christian burial. His dream had come true.

In just a short few years later, there was another battle here but again the Roscommon men prevailed and the Irish were victorious. Here, there now stands a huge monument of a warrior on horseback, standing glorious, victorious and high above a modern roadway. He stands in memory of the three victories at this magical place.

6

UNA BHAN

A lady called Una Uí Bruin married a man called Taigh MacDermott who was a Chieftain of Morlurg, an area in North Roscommon that included Lough Cé. One day, as she was nursing her first-born young son, an old beggar woman came to her door carrying a starved-looking baby that was probably a grandchild.

'God bless yourself and your lovely healthy child,' she said.

'And God bless you too,' Una replied.

'Will you give me a fistful of meal for the mother of this infant as she has no milk to feed him,' she said, holding out a tin cup.

Una dipped her hand in her meal-bin and brought out a small handful and put it in the cup.

'God bless you and thank you,' the old woman said. 'And would you have a small drop of milk for the little one to give him with the sparse strippings he sucked from his starving mother?'

'Be thankful you got the meal,' Una replied as she turned away.

'God bless you and your son Óg and may he and his children's children get their reward. One of them will be Una, like yourself and she will be remembered around Lough Cé, Keadue, Boyle, Ballyfarnon, Arigna and all Moylurg and all Roscommon forever.' And with that the old beggar turned on her heel and walked away. Una closed the door and thought no more about it. However, that night and every night thereafter she dreamt about the old woman and the hungry child. Eventually she told her husband. In order to allay her anxiousness he said it was tidings of good fortune for any grandchild of Óg who would be called Una. The good news became family lore.

Óg married young and had four sons in the following four years. Twenty-one years later all four married a year apart when each one was twenty-one years old. The oldest, Tómas, had three sons over the next the next four years. Padraig, the second son, had two sons, while Will, the third son, had one son. Then Dermot, the youngest, married and the following year all four families were blessed with baby daughters born in the same week. All four were called Una as all of them expected great fortune from their child as foretold by the beggar woman.

One child was dark-haired with brown eyes and she was called Una Dubh (black). Another had bright red hair and blue eyes and was called Una Dearg (red). The third had brown hair and green eyes and she was called Una Donn (brown). The last of the four babies was very fair with big bright beautiful blue eyes and she was called Una Bhan (white/fair).

Now, the wise druids always said that when a child is born there are four life paths left out for that person, and fate, fortune, faith and their own decisions will decide which path is followed. From the start Una Bhan was blessed with very good looks, great intelligence, agility, physical strength and stamina. She played demurely with the girls but more often she mixed it with the boys, racing, sword fighting, wrestling, stone throwing or weight lifting. She liked to dress like a boy with her beautiful golden hair wound up under a rough cap and was never outdone. If, at any time, she was not getting her own way, she would, when it suited her, pull off her cap, spilling her beautiful golden tresses over her shoulders and suitably blink her long eyelashes. One way or another she always got her way.

Now, the first of four ways that Una Bhan could have led her life would be to use her many talents and education to help the poor county children to read and write and make better lives for themselves and their families. She did not choose this way.

The second way would have been to follow her fighting instincts, go on pretending to be a boy, go to war with the army and die gloriously in battle. She did not choose this way.

The third way would be to be a good dutiful and obedient daughter, look after her younger siblings, help her mother with household chores, always be friendly to the neighbours and finally, marry the man her father selected. She did not choose this way.

Alas, her day of destiny arrived when she met Tómas Láidir Costello (Big Tómas Costello) tall, tawny, and trustworthy with a lovely manner and a broad, beaming, friendly come-hither smile to die for. She was totally smitten. Her mind was never her own again. She loved him more that anything in the world. She was ecstatic every moment in his arms. And – oh! – his lips, no words would be adequate to describe them. She pined every waking moment without him. She dreamt every sleeping moment about him. She was no longer herself but only part of him. He felt the same; they were the perfect match made in heaven. He proposed marriage, she blissfully accepted, and Tómas Láidir asked her father for her hand in marriage.

Her father thought he was unsuitable as he was from a socially inferior family. Perhaps he might consider him for any other of his daughters, but Una Bhan was the favoured one, the one who would be remembered forever. No, it would never happen. 'Go away Tómas Láidir,' was his reply.

'Ask again,' Una Bhan said, as she struggled to catch her breath from fright, fear and utter disappointment.

Una Bhan pleaded with her father. She told him she was in love. She flashed her eyelashes. She called him Dadsy-Wadsy. She reminded him of all their loving times, when he helped her take her first steps, when he tickled her, when he chased her round the table, when he showed her how to shoot an arrow, but all to no avail. He would not agree to the marriage.

Tómas Láidir went back the next day and asked again for her hand. Again he was refused.

'Ask one more time,' Una Bhan said.

'This is the last time,' Tómas Láidir muttered.

The next day he asked again, adding that this was the last time of asking. He was refused again. He went east across the Shannon at Drumboylan deciding never to return.

'I will never be humiliated again,' he said to himself. 'I can and will live without her. There are better fish in the sea.'

However, he was not able to sleep, he was not able to eat, he was not able to take any interest in anything; everything reminded him of Una Bhan. He could see her face in every flower, in every tree, in every stream, in every flying bird and even when he closed his eyes he could still see her. This went on for three days and three nights. He was losing his mind. On the fourth day he was not able to bear it any more. He decided to face her father again and if he refused again, he would come back by night and carry her away.

Meanwhile, Una Bhan paddled out in a little boat to the rock on Lough Cé. She sank the little boat, climbed the rock to where her ancestors first fell in love, returned that love to the God of Water and paid their debts to the Gods who created Lough Cé by dying for love. She was buried there and like the beggar woman said she will be remembered forever, but not in the way her father expected.

When Tómas Láidir finally returned and found out what happened he cursed himself for not returning sooner, he cursed her father for slighting him so and killing the lovely Una Bhan. He swam out to the rock, climbed up to her grave and laid beside it through the day and night in his wet clothes. He next morning he had great difficulty breathing and before the sun appeared out of the morning mists, he was dead. As her father was so devastated, he agreed to let Tómas Láidir be buried beside his darling Una Bhan, in eternal love.

LOUGH FUNCHEON, THE VANISHING LAKE AND THE FAIRIES

This is where the Goddess Danu, sometimes known as Dana, fought a hand-to-hand battle with the Fir Bolg giant Unch. It was not a lake then, but a dry sloping plane with a swallow hole in the middle that drained the whole area. The battle raged for a long time, with the nimble magical Dana running rings round the mighty Unch. Growing frustrated, as she knew he would, Unch made a last despairing lounge at Dana. She dropped to the ground and he flew over her, head first into the swallow hole. The swallow hole was an underground river that led all the way to the Shannon, six miles away. Now, Unch had a big head and big shoulders but the widest part of him was his giant backside. When he came to a narrow part of the tunnel, his head and shoulders got through but he got stuck at the hips. As the water could no longer get through it built up behind him and soon formed Lough Funcheon, named after Unch. At this stage, Unch called out to Dana, 'Don't leave me here as I will starve.' Dana took pity on him and said that although he could never leave the tunnel, every twenty years or so he could sit on the ledge above and have a great feed of passing fish. After the feast, he would have to resume his position, blocking the tunnel. Unch had to agree as he was under her spell. That is why, every twenty years or so, Lough Funcheon runs dry in a matter of hours. This is when Unch is having lunch. When this happens, fish are stranded in little pools and people and animals catch and devour most of them. However, when Unch has finished his meal he has to return to his position and the lake quickly returns to its natural size. In the future, as in the past, this phenomenon will puzzle many people and there will be 'Piseógs' superstitions and stories about it. Now you know. After this, Dana had to rush away on the north wind, going south, that took her to a place called Bóthar Buí (Yellow Road) on the Cork/Kerry border to fight another Fir Bolg giant. This was supposed to be a fight of single hand-to-hand combat but when she arrived, two Fir Bolg giants grabbed her by the breasts and pulled off her nipples. Immediately the nipples turned into mountains, burying the giants beneath them. Ever since, those mountains are known as Dana's Bosoms.

THE MORRIGAN, POOKA, BANSHEE, LEPRECHAUN AND THE LITTLE PEOPLE

The Magic Morrigan of the two spears was one of the Tuatha Dé Danann. Morrigan was a clever woman who lived with her two sons near the Cave of Cats. She taught her sons to make spears from oak saplings that would be about as high as a man and a half. The narrow end would be as thick as a man's wrist. She whittled the narrow end to a very sharp point. Those spears were then kept in the thatch near the fire for a year and a day to dry out and harden. They were the very best weapons of that time for hunting or war. Others tried to make similar spears but they never turned out as good as hers.

When she was an old woman, some enemies decided to kidnap her and force her to show them how to make the spears. To this end, two warriors with well-trained hounds watched her house from a distance until her sons went hunting. When they were sure that they would not return they approached the house. Just about that time the old woman decided to go outside for a call of nature. As she was now very old and feeble she took a spear in each hand to use as walking sticks. When the enemies saw her hobbling out, they set the dogs on her. Coming fast the dogs leaped upon her. She held onto the spears that rested on the ground and directed their points into the leaping dog's bellies. The hounds fell, yelping in the throws of death. The old woman was bowled over and rolled into undergrowth and down to the gully. Just then, an almost snow-white hare jumped from the undergrowth and ran past the gaping kidnappers.

'The magic Morrigan has killed our dogs and turned into a hare,' they cried, as they fled in terror. Did she turn into a hare? What do you think? She will certainly be around for a long, long time, maybe forever. This nearly white hare, that may be able to turn back into the Morrigan, can visit a person's cows on May morning and take the cream from their milk for that year. May morning is 1 May (Lady Day). It is even worse if a neighbour, who is out early on May morning, shoos the hare onto some other farm, for then, that person's cows may have double cream on their milk for the year. Of course, if the hare sees anybody ploughing or working with clay in preparation for sowing, she will put a curse on the worker and the crop with terrible results: the crop may fail, have a great many weeds or be very poor in quality and quantity. The May Day clay worker may have an accident, get sick, have a sick animal or child or even die before the year is out.

The pooka is a magic, mischievous animal with the legs of a wolf-hound and the body of a horse. He is able to run along under the ground and rise up under an unsuspecting man as he walks and carry him away. The man has no control so the pooka can take him anywhere. Sometimes he can throw him in a stream or a ditch or even in a cow-dung, or take him miles away. He might even deposit him in the bed of another man's wife. That is what they say anyhow!

The leprechaun is a tiny bearded man who sings, mends little boots, and drinks mountain dew from a tiny jug and minds pots of gold. He is very devious and only ever speaks in limericks. When anybody is lucky enough to see and catch a Leprechaun they can only hold him as long as they keep their eyes on him because if the person glances away, even for a second, the leprechaun will disappear. Many will try but nobody will ever get the crock of gold or a

drink for that matter. There will be many stories about men who nearly got the gold but at the last minute the leprechaun always managed to do some trick to get his captor to look around and then disappeared leaving the robber distraught.

For good or evil, the little people are always with us but are seldom visible. They are tiny, wispy people who like to sing, play tiny harps and dance. They sometimes travel in fairy blasts and like the direction of the wind are completely unpredictable. Beware their presence. They bring good or bad luck and if one disturbs them or their habitat their retribution can be terrible. If you build your house on one of their places they will make it impossible to live there and if you disturb them while sowing a crop, it will either not grow at all or the yield will be dismal. In some places where families emigrated or died out, the fairies may have been responsible. Wherever there is a lone white thorn tree, they make a home and woe betide anyone who cuts down that tree. They may send a stoat to kill all their hens, ducks, geese, turkeys and young lambs. All that can be done in retribution is to sow another thorn tree but the bad luck will last until it is full-grown, which could take up to forty years. However, protection for future generations is vital, even if one's own life is doomed to bad luck. Sometimes the little people lead men astray on their way home so that they cannot find the right road and may be travelling in circles for hours. If this happens one must take off one's coat and put it on inside out. This fools them and breaks their spell.

And what about the banshee? Ah! She is different. She stands about two foot high and has long golden hair that she is forever combing. If anybody disturbs her she may follow him or her and throw her comb at them. Being struck with her comb is usually fatal. The only way to escape her is to cross a stream, as she cannot follow. Her only purpose in life, if she is alive, is to comb her hair and to keen very loudly for deaths in certain families. This may make the families in question feared, admired or even despised. Some claim that her keening is an indication that the recent deceased has reached heaven but others, for whom she does not keen, may claim that it is the Devil rejoicing loudly at another arrival to his abode. What else but the Devil could make such unearthly sounds? Those opinions may change from generation to generation and may sometimes lead to fights or even feuds. Her keening will sometimes be embarrassing for families when one of their members conceived outside the blanket may be keened, even though he appears to belong in another family. Her keening takes place in dark lonely places as near as possible to the family homestead. Since the electric light arrived she is finding it difficult to find such dark places, as there is manmade light throughout the country, throughout the night.

9

THE MONSTER
OF LOUGH REE

The legend of the Monster of Lough Ree has always been, but smart modern people said it could not be true, as the lake was not deep enough to hide a monster. Moreover, they said that those who claimed to have seen it were probably poitín makers who were under the influence or were trying to scare off the police or customs men. The clever monster was not impressed so he presented himself to three sober clergymen of impeccable character in the 1950s. They described him as being a giant eel-like creature about two and a half feet thick and up to forty or fifty feet long. For the few minutes that they saw him he had his head and four bodily loops above the water. They thought he had a lump on his head and mouth and teeth like a pike. Controversy reigned for a time but the real story never came to light.

Another story about the monster dates from a hundred years before that. Two brothers from Knockcrockery, Mick and Pat, said they saw the monster late one night when they were passing by the lake, looking out toward Quaker Island. Locals ignored this sighting, as the brothers were well-known poitín makers and drinkers who plied their trade between the islands and all along the west side of the lake. However, two Englishmen heard about it and decided to investigate. Their names were Percival and Donald. Both of them were related to well-known, brave, worldwide explorers, and by virtue of their fear of any danger and inability to achieve much, they were somewhat despised by their families. Percival and Donald decided to make their names by capturing the Lough Ree Monster. To this end, they contacted Mick and Pat and employed them as guides and advisers. Mick introduced them to his brother-in-law, Tom, and his wife, Mary, who had a house with a spare room where Percival and Donald could board for only £1 each per day. They were lucky to get lodgings so near the lake!

Pat advised them to go to his brother-in-law, Joe, the black-smith, and get him to make a giant hook. At that time, the local forge was the only sort of leisure centre available to male laya-bouts, newsmongers, gabsters and nosy backbiters. There was always news and action there, and in order to keep the fair side of the blacksmith, those fellows would help with sledging, fit-ting iron tyres on cart wheels or helping with young horses. Mick advised the Englishmen that their adventure needed to be kept strictly secret and that nothing would remove the hanger-ons from the forge, only free drink. Mick suggested to Percival that a £5 float for a free bar in the local shebeen (illegal pub) would empty the forge so that they and the blacksmith could get down to business. Percival complemented Mick on his shrewdness and paid the money. He did not know that the shebeen was owned by Pat's uncle.

Now, Joe, Percival, Donald, Pat and Mick got to work. The hook had to be designed and made properly. A six-foot-long crowbar an inch thick was selected. Joe heated it in the fire, two feet from one end, and he and Pat lifted it on to the anvil with big pinchers. Then Joe beat it into a lovely hook. It was heating time again so that the point of the hook could be beaten and barbs cut out with a chisel and turned so that the hook would hold fast to the captured creature. This was then cooled and the other end heated white and beaten flat before a hole was punched in it, to hold a twenty-yard long chain.

Just about that time, another brother-in-law, Tim, had a litter of little piglets and Pat acquired one for bait on the giant hook. Pat

only charged Percival a pound for the pig. The chain was anchored to a tree on land and the hook with the dead pig on it was brought out by boat seventeen yards and then dropped from the far side of the boat so that it hung nine feet down over the side. As they were afraid of the monster, they anchored the boat there and returned to land in another boat. Mick owned the boats but he only charged £1 per boat per day. The Englishmen were rich. They watched from the shore for several hours and when their patience wore out they went out and pulled up the hook. The pig was gone.

'Well, doesn't that beat Banagher,' said Mick.

'The bloody monster is as clever as a Christian. We will have to secure the bait better.' They tried again the next day and this time they tied the pig on with a rope. It did no good and when they pulled up the hook there was nothing there but the rope. This went on every day, with more and better ropes used until all twelve of the litter of little pigs were gone. Every night Pat, Mick, and Tim procured expensive poitín for Percival and Donald, who drank themselves to sleep.

As they were eating their breakfast on the eleventh morning, Mary, who always had too much to say, asked, 'Are ye going to feed another pig to the pike today?'

The penny dropped with Donald. 'Is that what has been eating out bait? There must be no monster at all. We have been wasting our time. We will not go on the lake again. How much is our bill? We will be leaving today.'

'What sort of an Óinseach [fool] are you woman?' said Tom. 'How could pike get near the bait, sure the monster would eat them too. You're talking nonsense like always.' But the damage was done. The Englishmen were onto the ruse. That's when Pat and Mick arrived. Tom, interrupted often by his wife, told of the morning's conversation.

'Well, isn't that the best ever you heard,' said Pat, 'but don't worry, we'll catch him yet. We need a bigger pig with several ordinary fish hooks inserted in him and then, every pike that bites him will get caught and make a better bait altogether for the monster.'

'I am not convinced,' said Percival. 'I have lost faith in you, your bait, your boats and the monster. In fact, I'm sceptical as to whether there ever was a monster.'

'Didn't you tell me that your brother climbed the highest mountain in Europe, Mattie's Horn?' asked Mick, 'and I bet he didn't give up just when he could see the top.'

'It's the Matterhorn,' said Percival with a condescending smile at the ignorant peasant. But he was stung by the suggestion that he was a quitter or that he was less than his brother, the mountaineer.

'I suppose we could give it one more go if you are agreeable, Donald, and if another pig is available.'

By sheer luck, another brother-in law had arrived from Gaily Bay with a bigger pig in an ass's cart. Not only that, in spite of his great size, he was prepared to sell him for just £2. Luck struck again when a stranger turned up with fifty special hooks to implant in the pig and he even had short lines to attach to the hooks and to the big hook.

'It looks as if fate is on our side this time,' said Donald. The stage was set for the final trap to catch the monster.

The pig was killed. The hooks were inserted and the pig was tied to the big hook. All was loaded on to the boat. It was rowed out the seventeen yards. The pig, complete with big hook and fifty small hooks, was dropped over the side. Then all hell broke loose! The chain became taut and was wrenched over the end of the boat nearly overturning it. The tree that the chain was anchored to shook as great pressure was put on it. Then everything went quiet. Tim and Tom who were on the shore pulled in the slack chain. There was nothing on the end of it and the big inch thick, hook had been straightened out. Pat, Percival and Donald who had been in the first boat, was busy hiding their embarrassment at what the fright caused. Mick was in the other boat with a bottle on his head. There was a monster after all. Everybody but the English were surprised. Pat and Mick did much less boating on the lake thereafter, and Percival and Donald had the best fishy story of all time.

What none of them knew was that a very long time ago this monster was not confined to Lough Ree, but roamed about the Midlands, as it was mostly shallow Lakeland then. The River Suck was a mile wide then but was very shallow. The monster, whose name was Sneaky, had two tusk-like teeth that he could conceal in his mouth but that he could stick out a foot in distance when necessary. That was how he dug burrows. He could also purse his lips and squirt water with speed, power and accuracy for a distance of a hundred yards. He had a burrow six or eight feet below the bottom of the river going all the way from the Shannon to near Dysart.

Very powerful druids in the north heard of the monster and decided to kill him in case any of their enemies got control of him. To this end, they made a magic potion and fed it to Bran, an Irish wolfhound, every day for a year and a day. As well as the potion they fed him an ever-increasing amount of meat so that by the end of the year he was consuming a whole cow every day. At the end of that time, the potion and the meat had made him grow two hundred feet tall, with legs a hundred feet long. From his snout to the tip of his tail, the distance was five hundred feet. They sent him to dig out and kill the monster. The monster heard him coming and dived into his burrow that went under the Suck. The dog smelt him and, standing in Creagh near Ballinasloe, he started to root up the burrow with his paws. He sent water, muck and rocks flying and this deluge landed in Tachmaconnell and started to create the Breole Hills. As he tore up the burrow he backed away along its length, eventually creating all the Breole Hills. Just when Bran was about to grab him, Sneaky raised his head and squirted out a fierce jet of water into Bran's eyes. While

the dog yelped and rubbed his eyes with his paws, the monster escaped down river and into a side burrow that ran beneath the newly formed Breole Hills. The dog gave up and slowly headed home. As he was very tired after his exertions he had a long sleep for a week on the high ground near Four Roads. This was after he had killed and eaten a cow in Dysart.

When Sneaky realised that the dog was gone he got cocky and thought he was great and that he could do anything he liked. He quickly swam down the Suck and up the Shannon, feeling like the master of the Lakelands. As he went, he grabbed and ate huge numbers of salmon, trout, bream, perch, pike and eels. For sport, he occasionally caught a salmon, tossed him in the air and caught him coming down. Another time, he would squirt water into the air causing a great ark and creating a rainbow. Although he did not like bird meat, he would sometimes use his squirt power to shoot down a passing seagull, swan, snipe or duck, just for sport. He might also severely hurt, with his water pistol, any otter or other lake dweller that came within his range, again, just for sport. The other creatures did not see the funny side and avoided him as best they could.

At that time, the Shannon, like the Suck, was very wide and very shallow. Just as Sneaky reached Ballyleague he looked up and spotted Bran who was ambling along. As he had a burrow running under the Shannon most of the way to Athlone and he felt invincible and mischievous so he squirted a jet of water at Bran's backside, knocking a yelp out of him and then retreated down his burrow laughing.

Bran got extremely angry and attacked the burrow with twice the vigour of the last dig. Again he sent rocks, muck and water to the clouds. This muck landed where the White Mountain is now. As he proceeded down the river, he got evermore angry and threw the dredged matter further and further. Just about the time that he had created Sliabh Bhan and Lough Ree, he got a brainwave. He would put out his paw a further hundred yards, press down into

the burrow and push the monster back into his open mouth. The
ruse worked and as the monster got pushed out of the burrow Bran
opened his mouth to eat it. He wasn't quick enough, propelled by
a great swish of his tail, Sneaky came from the water at great speed
and before Bran could close his teeth on him, Sneaky was gone
down his neck and into his belly. Sneaky swam about biting every
thing he saw causing great pain and discomfort to the dog. Bran
tried to vomit him out but he was too strong a swimmer and just
continued to bite. Eventually poor Bran fell down in pain and was
drowned in the lake he had just made.

When Bran stopped moving, Sneaky just swam up his gullet and
out to freedom. He had won again but he had got a terrible fright.
When he had looked into the dog's mouth and seen all those sharp
teeth, he thought he had reached his doom. Only for a very lucky
flash of genius he would have been eaten alive. He would never
take a chance like that again.

Willo-the-Wisp was an unusual type of fairy. He had three unique
features. Firstly, he could be a small red light that was always fifty
or more yards from any who saw it. Secondly, he had a strange
call, a sort of 'toohooha' that was like a ventriloquist in so much as
it was impossible to say exactly from whence it came. Thirdly, he
could manifest himself as a sort of shimmering half-ghost.

One night, as Sneaky ambled along near Rindoon he saw the
red light and immediately squirted water at it with great force.
As it was quite near he was confident of hitting it. A funny thing
happened, instead of hitting the light the water turned back and
hit him in the eye. He got mad and squirted harder. The water hit
him harder in the other eye. When he stopped squirting he heard
the toohooha but he could not figure out where it was coming
from. He twisted and turned, and turned and twisted until his
head spun and hit a rock that was sticking out of the water. It put
a bump on his forehead that swelled up into an ugly lump that he

has to this day. As he recovered from the daze caused by the bump he saw the shimmering ghost sort of sliding along the water. By now he was very angry so he swam and swam until he was going at a great speed and he was closing on the ghost. So intent was he in pursuit that he never noticed when the ghost seemed to fly a little higher. In a splash he was grounded on the Rindoon peninsula. Not only that, but every bit of him was out of the water and that left him powerless except to thrash about on land. Now he saw the red light fifty yards down the shore, while the ghost was fifty yards out on the water. Then the toohooha started again and it seemed to say, 'tooyooarbeeenpuuniisshhdfoorhhuurrttiingm-maanywaatrfrreends'.

Before this, Sneaky was always to able to make ten loops of his long body above the water but from that day he could only ever make four loops and that is what the clergymen saw. Sneaky was so terrified that he thrashed and turned so much that he made a slip-way back down to the water and eventually slid into Lough Ree. The slide he made was later used by boat builders to launch their new crafts. It is still there, behind the ruined castle.

In order to avoid Willo-the-Wisp, and not wishing to be fooled, scared, bumped or grounded, he decided he would live quietly alone in his burrow, far below the river and only come out to eat, splash and play in the water on very dark nights. Then even if he was seen fleetingly, people would think it was a hallucination or some trick of the little people. However, as his name and nature was Sneaky, and he was afraid of being forgotten altogether, he took a chance with the clergymen and showed himself. Perhaps he will do it again soon!

10

TWO ROCKS

There was once a young king in Cruachan who had inherited his crown from his father and who expected, in due time, to hand it on to his eldest son. His name was Alli. He married Onna, a beautiful red-haired princess from Boyle, out near Lough Gara. They were blissfully happy for the first year of their marriage, a little bit concerned the second year and nearly alarmed the third year. There was also talk around the realm of bad luck, witches' spells, old grudges, old curses, old killings and cruelty. What was causing all this trouble? The princess was not showing any signs of pregnancy; in fact, she was getting thinner. Witches, wise women, wonder workers and wandering bards were consulted but all to no avail. Those magic workers were afraid to offer help or advice because the same thing had happened several generations before, and those who tried to help were blamed when their efforts failed and some were severely punished by imprisonment, beatings, exile, and, in one case, death. Memories were long among the wise.

Some years before this, a funny little wandering bard with spiky red hair, a piercing eye and a magic harp appeared near Lough Cé. Nobody knew where he came from or remembered him growing up, and any who asked were silently stared down by his piercing eye and asked no more. His name was Sharp Eye. On his harp he played wonderful magical enchanting airs that nobody had heard before and most people believed that he got those airs and the magic harp from the fairy gods. Some said that he was a spoiled druid, as he knew a lot of magic. Over the years he drifted and played all across Maigh Luirg and Maigh Ai, finally arriving at the White Mountain. He said to his host family that he would like to live the rest of his life on the mountain. They said this was impossible as he had no house and no permanent water supply.

The next day he climbed the mountain until he came to a great oak tree, standing tall and stately but that was decaying on its north side. Sharp Eye sat on a rock high above the oak and played a strange eerie tune. With every note the wind got stronger and stronger, putting more and more pressure on the oak. Eventually the ground beside the tree began to shudder and then the great roots began to come up out the earth on one side as the oak fell slowly towards the ground. It came to rest a few feet from the earth, held up by a few tenacious roots that refused to budge. Water immediately gushed from a spring in the hole left by the roots and made a stream down the mountain. The tree had fallen in such a way that it was not too difficult to make a habitable and reasonably comfortable residence beneath its trunk. This the bard did.

Alli, the king, remembered what his father had told him: 'No matter how expensive or beautiful a cravat you wear, none will ever equal the loving arms of your son around your neck.' So, as a last resort, the royal couple approached Sharp Eye and asked for his help. He said he would help. If the royal couple would come to live near him for the life of one moon and drink daily from the well, while he played strange airs on his harp, it would solve their problem. They agreed because, although they were sceptical, desperation trumped doubt. The couple and their small entourage stayed with friends at the base of the mountain.

On the first six mornings they drank from the well while the bard strummed his harp. On the seventh morning, after they had drank from the well, they had to kill a drake, sprinkle his blood on the stream and then burn the drake in a prepared fire. The following six days they had only to drink from the well but on the fourteenth day, after their drink, they had to kill a cock, sprinkle his blood on the stream and burn him in the fire. The following six days they just had a drink but on day twenty-one they had to kill a gander, sprinkle his blood and burn him as before. At each burning, all those present were encouraged to whoop loudly while jumping over or through the fire. That is, all except the royal couple. When the gander was burning some jumpers got scorched as the goose grease sent the flames higher. The drinking continued until the twenty-eighth day and then a wild boar, that had previously been captured, was killed and roasted on a spit over the fire. He was not burned or buried, instead everyone had a great feast, Sharp Eye played lovely airs on his magic harp and all were happy.

Alli took Sharp-Eye aside and asked him how his magic worked.

'Do you not trust me?' asked Sharp Eye.

'Of course I trust you,' said the king, 'and I have total faith in the magic of you, your magic harp and your magic well. I am confident it will work and I will be forever grateful to you.' But, as he said it, there was a slight falter in his voice. Sharp Eye eyed him and said, 'By the life of my life, my harp, my music and my well, you can be certain that the magic will work better than you expect and that its fruits will be remembered long after you and your kingdom are forgotten.'

'How will I pay you?' asked the king.

'When I want payment I will ask for it,' Sharp Eye replied.

'Alright,' said the king.

The magic worked. The queen fell pregnant and was delighted. Sharp Eye was delighted. The people were delighted. The king was delighted, but also thoughtful. The royal party returned triumphant to Cruachan. There was joy throughout the realm especially in the White Mountain area, because by royal decree taxes were reduced in that area for a year and a day. Sharp Eye was a hero there. But elsewhere, others were jealous and some suspicious.

Well, the pregnancy was not just successful, it was doubly successful, and they had twin boys. There was just one thing that bothered the new parents. The experienced and trusted old midwife who delivered the twins seemed to be struck dumb as she handed them to their mother who was only just recovering from the delirium of birth pains. When others entered the room moments later the queen was happily nursing her two babies but the old midwife was lying on the floor stone dead. Neither the queen, nor anybody else knew which twin arrived first, so nobody knew which should be heir to the throne. Was it Ferdi or was it Fionn?

Everybody was happy and the boys grew big, strong, fleet of foot and wise. Soon, they would be men. They both looked like their mother except that Fionn was flaxen haired while Ferdi had hair as black as ebony.

When the boys were eighteen years old the king decided to set them a task to see which should inherit the crown. At that time in Cruachan they used to have passage tombs for kings, but Alli thought that they were inadequate. He asked that they both go throughout the realm and find the biggest possible stone that could be used as a cap for his passage tomb, when his time came. When they found such a stone, they were to raise it on uprights so that a tomb could be dug out and built beneath.

Fionn headed south to Uí Maine country while Ferdi went north to Maigh Ai, his mother's place. They both took ten comrades on horseback with them. They also had much to barter in tools, weapons, jewellery, knives and artefacts made from stone, timber, bone, tooth and bronze.

Fionn criss-crossed the county, searching Strokestown, Rooskey, Tarmonbarry, Ballagh, Four Mile House, Ballymoe, Oran, Fuerty, Roscommon, Knockcrockery, Ballyforan, Ballybay, Tachmaconnell, Creagh and Moore. Finally, he found just what he was looking for at a place called Mehanbee, in the parish of Drum. It was a great flat rock, ten feet wide, fifteen feet long and two feet thick. It probably weighed twenty-five tons. It would surely win him the prize, if he could raise it six feet and put uprights under it.

To this end, he employed 120 strong young men. As he was interviewing for the positions, a tiny man, barely two feet tall asked for a job.

'How could one so small and weak be any use lifting such a big rock?' asked Fionn.

'My name is Weakness, and I am not big or strong,' said the little man, 'but I can be more lethal than any of those big fellows.' Everybody laughed and Fionn dismissed the little man who shuffled away muttering to himself. The newly hired team cut and fashioned twenty nine-inch thick oak crowbars that were ten-feet long. Then they dug a nine-inch wide and nine-inch deep groove from under the rock. They put fulcrums of smaller flat stones along one side of the giant rock. Then, all crowbars, having been slid in over the fulcrums into the prepared groove, were used in unison, with four men handling each and five more pulling on ropes attached to the top of the poles. On their first effort, one side of the rock was raised nearly a foot. It was quickly propped up by the other twenty men who were standing by with timbers at the ready. Then all moved to the other side and repeated the operation. They kept repeating the process, moving from side to side and propping as they went. The higher they went the more difficult it became to get the necessary fulcrums and props. However, they eventually had the rock on timbers six feet above the ground. Now they had to find transport and erect six strong flat-stone uprights. They found them fairly close by and rolled them on the crowbars to the required location beside the rock. When this was done, the fulcrums were again utilised, the huge rock was raised slightly. The standing stones were heaved upright into slots in the clay, going down to the gravel base with their tops just beneath the rock. The tops of the standing stones were chipped until they were level. Stones were hammered in around the base of the standing stones to keep them firmly in place. Now the timber props were removed and the rock lowered onto the standing stones. This was done first on one side then on the other. When all the timbers were removed the twenty-five-ton

rock was standing on the upright stones, six feet above ground. It was a wonderful sight to see and everybody was very impressed with Fionn's engineering and management skills.

Now the moment of truth arrived. Who was going to go under the rock and start digging for the passage-tomb? Fionn went right in and started digging. The sky did not fall; neither did the rock nor any of the standing stones. Soon everybody was helping and the tomb was finished within a few days. They called the tomb, Giant Leaba (Giant Bed).

Fionn was confident that he had won as there was unlikely to be another rock like that anywhere. And even if there was, things might not have gone as well for his brother. As it was late in the day, they did not go far before setting up camp for the night.

Meanwhile, Ferdi had searched Castlerea, Ballinlough, Loughglinn, Fairymount, Frenchpark, Elphin, Kilmore, Croghan, Ballinameen, Castlerea, Ardcarn, Keadue, Ballinafad, Creevagh and Boyle. He had seen many rocks but none suitable for his purpose until he found just what he wanted in Drumanoghan, near Lough Gara, in the parish of Boyle. As he was a twin brother of Fionn and they had grown, learned, played, fought, raced, hunted, sang, drank and slept together all their lives, he had the same way of thinking and so he solved the problem of the rock in the same way. He got the same successful result. The only remarkable thing that happened was that one of those who turned up looking for a job from Ferdi was a fine-looking young girl.

'How could you, a mere girl work hard all day with those strong men?' Ferdi asked.

'My name is Female and I will have more to do with this enterprise than anyone else,' she replied. Here too, all the men laughed and the girl slunk away. No more was thought of it.

When the job was finished the local druid asked Ferdi if he could offer one pigeon as a good luck sacrifice on the top of the rock. Ferdi agreed and that is why the rock is called the Druid's Altar. Then Ferdi thanked his host, the King of Maigh Ai, gave him presents and decided to stay by Lough Gara for the night before he returned to Cruachan.

After the twins, the royal couple had several more children and as each one arrived, Alli thought of the Sharp Eye, his music and his magic well and often wondered if he would ask for payment, and if so, what? About this time, Sharp Eye, who was now old and feeble, called to Cruachan to see the king and queen.

'I have come for my payment,' he said.

'Certainly,' said Alli, 'and what is it?'

'I want your first daughter, May the Fair, for now she is seventeen years old and I heard that the King of Meidh has asked for her hand in marriage, but I have first call,' he said.

'Never!' screamed the queen, as Alli just went pale and was lost for words. Sharp Eye stared at Alli and said, 'Are you going to dishonour your debt because of the hysterics of a woman?' Alli said nothing at first but when he looked at his wife he said, 'Ask for something reasonable.'

'The deal or nothing,' said Sharp Eye.

'But I will give you anything you ask for within reason,' said Alli.

'The deal or nothing,' shouted Sharp Eye again.

'Then it is nothing,' said Alli. Onna called the palace guards and ordered them to throw Sharp Eye out. As he was carried away, he continued to stare at Alli and said, 'So you think our deal is off, soon enough you'll see what it means to have no deal.' When the guards had him outside, they put him on his pony but he refused to move. So the guards mounted two horses, one on each side of him and marched Sharp Eye and his pony all the way back to his mountain home. There they dismounted, lifted him from his pony, threw him into his hut, closed the door and left, taking the pony with them. They never looked back, knowing that old Sharp Eye would not be able to follow without his pony. That night there was a fire in Sharp Eye's cabin. Nobody knew how it started, but some wondered, but he and his harp were consumed in the flames. The heat was so great that it cracked the rock beneath the spring and no water was ever seen there again. It was as if Sharp Eye, his stare, his harp, his music, his holy well and his house had never been!

When the royal couple heard this, Onna said, 'Good riddance.' Alli wondered.

Fionn and his men had slept in a clearing beside a stream in an oak wood. After breakfast they set off through the wood. The little two-foot-high man had climbed a tall tree and laid in wait. As Fionn was passing he jumped from above, came down fast, landed on Fionn's head and both fell dead on the ground. There was nothing anyone could do. His companions carried Fionn back to the prepared burial chamber and laid him there, a man in his own grave.

The next morning, after Ferdi and his men had breakfast and as they looked upon beautiful Lough Gara, they decided to have a swim before the journey. They stripped off, dived in and started to swim around. That's when they saw her – Female was swimming a little further out.

'Is there any among you who will race me to the far shore?' she asked. Three men, including Ferdi, shouted 'We will!' All four started swimming straight away. As Ferdi was the strongest swimmer he was able to go as fast as the girl but the space between them stayed the same. She was a very good swimmer. The other two men fell some way behind Ferdi. Suddenly a great whirlpool developed between the girl and Ferdi. Before he could react he was sucked down. The whirlpool abated after ten minutes, but, by then, Ferdi was floating face down on the surface. Female was nowhere to be seen. The others frantically pulled Ferdi ashore but he never breathed again. With his snow-white face and his jet-black hair he was like a sleeping god, but alas one that would never awaken. They interred him in the tomb beneath the Druid's Altar.

Months later, a sad and sorry royal couple visited Drumanoghan and saw the Druid's Altar above their beloved Ferdi. Their grief was almost unbearable but they both thought that the mighty stone was indeed a suitable monument for a king, even if he had not lived long enough to be king. It gave them some slight consolation.

Then they made the long journey all the way to Drum. They thought it strange that both gravestones were in places starting with Drum! Finally, they arrived at Mehanbee, Drum, and looked upon the grave of their other darling son, Fionn. Again the great stone was impressive and again they grieved that he did not live long enough to be king. Then it hit them, Sharp Eye had said that their firstborn would be remembered long after they and their kingdom would be forgotten. How right he was! The monuments are still there millennia later. Who won the competition? The tombs are still there. Come and judge if you dare!

11

SNAMH DHÁ EAN
– SWIM TWO BIRDS

After the episodes of the druids in Lough Cé, the Goddess Danu, also known as Dana, rewarded Oli and Ola by turning them into a beautiful swan and a beautiful duck for one hundred years. She gave them the task of travelling round in such a manner that they would mark out the margins of Roscommon. It was a journey that would take them 100 years as they were expected to swim most of the way, though occasional short flights were allowed. At the end of the task, they were made the leaders of the little people for all time.

They toured around Lough Cé, first taking in Ballinafad for two years, Ballyfarnon for four years and Keadue, Kilronan and Arigna for five years each. They spent some good times swimming around Inishatirra island in Drumharlow Lough after coming through Oakport Lough on their way from Lough Key. From there, they swam down Lough Alan to where it enters the Shannon. From there, they took leisurely trips into Coothall, Ardcarne and Tumna spending many seasons in each. All along there they established homes where our little people could live and get into the minds of any they encountered.

They arrived at Drumboylan and immediately noticed that this would be a historic place for Roscommon, as great things would one day happen there. They notified our little people to be on standby. A thousand years here or there is not much to the little people. Then they visited Croghan for a long time, as it would be famous. Killukin and Killamud each had the pleasure of their company for a long time.

Where the Shannon turns east they arrived at Aughrim and Kilmore and they had to sort of swim round those parishes. Then they swam up the Owenur River, lake and swamp all the way to Elphin, taking in Kiltrustan, Bumlin, Creve, Lissnuffy, Strokestown and Clonfinlough. This was a wonderful trip as the area was very variable and teeming with every sort of wildlife where people struggled to fight their corner. There were lovely eerie wooded places for our people to settle. This trip took several years.

When they got back to the Shannon they glided by Kilglass and Roosky, taking many moons for trips inland, even as far as Kilglass Lough, where they had some good times. Lough Forbes tempted them to tarry but Whitehall, Tarmonbarry, Kilbarry and Scramoge were calling and it was clear to Ola and Oli that Tarmonbarry would always be a very important crossing point.

Then, on they went to Ballyleague and the entrance to Lough Ree. They frolicked in the lake for many years and one day Sneaky the monster appeared and tried to eat them. They ran and flapped along the water but when he was gaining on them they took to the air. Sneaky spewed water after them and hit Oli in the tail, knocking feathers flying and causing him to fly sideways and lose altitude. Sneaky shrieked with laughter, as he knew that he would get in another shot before Oli had time to recover. He had not reckoned with Ola who was flying above and now dived down beak first and stabbed the monster in the eye. Sneaky was flabbergasted. No bird, fish, otter, or any creature other than the giant dog had ever had the audacity to attack him. Before he could recover his composure, Ola had swung back to the air and came up under the failing Oli, pulling him in over the Island of Inchena where Sneaky could not follow. There they landed to recover their strength and composure. Ever after, they kept a close lookout for monsters.

This somewhat spoiled the ambience of the lake so they drifted down to the rapids in Athlone where they went 'wh-e-e-e' among the white water. It was so good that they went back and did it again and again. They went on a race one each side of Long Island and Calves Island and nearly crashed into each other at the other end. It was a draw.

After many years they arrived at Shannonbridge, where there was a beautiful little island that intrigued them and they decided to stay a while. Every morning they had a race round the island. Although the swan could swim a little faster, he had to take a wider circle, as he needed deeper water. The duck, on the other hand, could take a shorter circle in shallower water. Sometimes the duck won the race while other times the swan won. They both enjoyed this sport immensely as they whooped and quacked and splashed in loud laughing boisterous merriment. Now people watching could not say 'see the two swans or see the two ducks', so they said 'Snamh Dá Ean' (Swim Two Birds) and that is how the island got its name. Of course the people did not know that they were not really seeing two birds, but two of our fairy people. Nor did they know that everyone who watched them became carefree Irish ever after.

As Ola and Oli swam around the island every day they were watched by Rena, a fox who, although he was able to get plenty of food, was partial to the taste of swan. Indeed, his descendants would always be known for their fondness of geese and swans and there would be many stories about their clever antics in goose and swan snatching. Once, when Rena was a cub, he watched a swan all day and succeeded in stealing up on her and grabbing her tail. Immediately there was a great flapping, hissing and squawking and the swan was gone, leaving the cub with a mouthful of feathers. He would be wiser the next time. He knew that he could match the swan on land, in water it would be much more difficult, but in the air, he had no chance at all. How could he get the lovely white swan that swam daily with a duck around the little island? He thought of a plan.

There was a small bush on the shore, about the size of a swan, just fifteen yards from the island. Over several days Rena gathered white feathers and when he had enough he stuck them on the little bush so that it looked like a swan. The next morning as Ola and Oli were swimming around the island as usual, they noticed the swan. They wondered why he never moved and wondered if he was sick and needed help. To this end, they swam over to him and just as they realised that he was a fake the fox jumped on Oli in the water. Surprised, Oli dived and tried to swim below the surface but the wily fox had broken his wing and now he was closing in for the kill. Ola, who had taken to the air, dived into the bush scattering feathers all around the fox and in the confusion that followed, Ola bit his tail and fluttered along the water feigning injury. Rena was mesmerised, and for a second was between two minds whether to chase the swan or the duck. The duck collapsed prostrate on the water, the fox decided that a duck was better than nothing so he swam that way. The duck took to the air and by then the injured swan was out in the safety of deep water. In great pain and with help from Ola, the injured swan staggered on to the island. There was a log there and when Oli placed his wing on it, the pain eased, indicating that if he could stay in this position for long enough the wing would heal. This he did for three weeks while he was waited on wing and webbed feet by Ola, who provided for all his needs and preened him daily to keep his feathers clean, white, comfortable and waterproof. The wing got better and the swan, the duck and the fox were wiser.

Ready to continue their journey once more, the swan and the duck arrived at the entrance to the river Suck and turned northwest into it. There were extensive lakelands and swamps all the way to Creagh and Ballinasloe. They had great times there with the water hens, hen harriers, snipes, grouse, lapwings, curlews, wild geese, mallards, widgeons and swans. In fact, they had a sort of regatta with races, diving, flying and singing contests. Even the fish joined in, jumping high out of the water. The final chorus was truly amazing with all the differing calls, whoops and quacks, not to mention the flapping, splashing and diving. It was a most joyous occasion, not only for the participants, but also for the landlubbers watching from the shore.

They followed the river by Tachmaconnell and on to Ballyforan. From there, they took a flight across Dysart to Lough Funcheon just to check if it was there. It was and they met many forest friends and forest creatures as the lake was then in the middle of a forest. On the way back they crossed Four Roads and, having again joined the river, they swam on to Athleague and Fuerty where the river was very wide and interspersed with many islands. There, again, there were huge numbers of birds, fish and animals from water and land. The craic was mighty.

On they went to Cregs, Cloverhill, Oran, Ballymoe and Ballintober. They went back and forth there for more than a year before reaching Castlerea with its underground springs bubbling up in the river and giving a jacuzzi effect. This was worth a long stay as jacuzzis were scarce then. They took in Ballinlough and Kiltullagh before flying to Loughglinn among the woods. They crossed Ballaghderreen on their way to Lough Gara and went by the Boyle river, back to Lough Cé.

The hundred years were spent and Ola and Oli reverted to form and became our fairy leaders, whizzing around on fairy blasts and playing with and among humans for all time.

12

OILEÁN NA SIÓGA
~ THE FAIRY ISLAND

The little Fairy Island, only one acre in size, is in Lough Ree just a hundred yards from the Roscommon shore at an inlet called Hudson Bay in the parish of Kiltoom.

When the Tuatha Dé Danann first arrived in Roscommon, the island was farther out as the water was higher. A small number of the little people, led by Airy, arrived on the wind at the swamp, heading for the high ground that is now a golf course. This high ground overlooked Lough Ree, near the edge of which was a little island that would soon be known as Fairy Island. However, the little people were waylaid by hundreds of Fir Bolgs led by Kinba. The group ducked and dodged for hours to tire the Fir Bolgs but they had reinforcements and when one lot were worn out they were replaced by fresh men. In the end, two of the little people were captured.

The Fir Bolgs were so excited when they caught the two that they let Airy and the rest of the little people escape back across the swamp that was becoming a bog. The swamp was too soft for the big Fir Bolgs to walk on so they could not follow. The Fir Bolgs all gathered around the two little folk to question them. This gave Airy a chance to reassemble his little band and surround the Fir Bolgs with a mighty wind that threatened to blow them into the Shannon. He would have blown them into the river but the two captives would be drowned with them. Therefore he had to negotiate.

Kinba refused point blank to negotiate so Airy increased the wind and blew them down the hill nearer the lake. Kinba still refused to parley so the little people blew harder but they could not bear to injure the captives. After several hours bracing against the cold wind, Kinba relented and agreed to talk.

He still refused to release the two little people but he said he would keep them as hostages. He would lock them up but they would be fed and looked after as long as the rest of the little people gave up magic and obeyed the king of the Fir Bolgs. Of course, Airy could not agree as none of the little people could ever live in captivity, nor could they be subject to any deity.

Airy then suggested that, for the freedom of the two, he would help the king in battle with the Firmorians. They were the other tribe in Roscommon at that time. Kinba considered this; he would love to be rid of the fierce Firmorians. They had been fighting with his people for generations but they had no magic and now he had two of the magic people. He was not about to let them go. He said he would only agree if he still held the captives. Airy could not sacrifice the captives so than plan had to be dropped.

Airy then suggested to Kinba to let the captives live on the little island if they agreed never to leave it, no matter what happened. This was agreed by both sides and the two fairies, Ay and By, were marooned on the little island.

Now, the Fir Bolgs knew something about the island that our people did not know. When Lough Ree was being formed, this little island appeared when Sneaky, the monster of the lake, dug a deep hole for himself and tossed up the island. The God of Land and the God of Water had an argument about it. The God of Water did not want it there at all because it was not in his original plans but the God of Land insisted that it be kept. Finally, they agreed to leave it, for what they said was a short time. They agreed that it would sink an inch every hundred years and, eventually, it would disappear beneath the water. The Fir Bolgs knew this and they were prepared to wait to drown our two little fairies.

But the Earth God intervened, and, as the island sunk, so did the water table so that it only ever went under water in times of very high floods, maybe once in fifty or a hundred years. Even then, our little people survived, as there were always a few trees with their heads above water, where they could shelter until the floods receded. But they were always worried that sooner or later the trees would be covered and they would be lost. Another problem they had was that they were not able to see far enough across the lake as their home was on such low ground.

One day, Ay found a way to solve those two problems. In the eighteenth century there was a young man called Denis who lived on the hill overlooking the island. His house was above where the Hudson Bay Hotel is now. He was courting a beautiful girl called Mary who lived near Gailey Bay. This was a secret romance, as her father had someone else in mind for her and certainly would not give her in marriage to Denis, a man who lived on a sandy hill. He went twice a week by boat to see her. He went in the evenings so it was always dark when he arrived and when he returned, yet he always managed to come between the island and the reeds. Ay and By watched his movements for a long time and then made a plan.

Our two little people were able to create small whirlwinds on the island or small currents round the island. Occasionally they might send a meitheal – a working crowd to help in some emergency – then they could create considerable whirlwinds or currents. They gathered a meitheal and one night, when he was coming home, they created a whirlwind and current and ran his boat aground on the island.

When they had him there, they put him into a deep sleep and, by morning, they had convinced him to build a tower on the island so that he could put a light on top of it to guide nightly mariners. The very next day, he went to work and got help from others to bring out stones and start the tower. When he had it built, he put a replica of his boat in stone on top of it and he put a hole in the stone to hold a lamp standard. That evening, he put a light on the tower before he went on his romantic mission. When he proposed elopement to the lovely Mary, she accepted and he rowed her back to his home directed by the light and serenaded by Ay and By with their tiny voices.

In return for the tower that Denis built, that will always be well above high water, they made sure that Denis and Mary lived happily ever after and that all who passed by or visited the tower would feel their presence and have them in their dreams.

13

QUEEN MEABH
OF CONNAUGHT

Queen Meabh was married to a descendent of Ashling and Hau called Ailill, who was King of Connaught. Meabh was the daughter of the High King Laoghaire and she will always be known as Queen Meabh of Connaught.

Her personality may be deduced from the fact that had her own stone-sculpted Sheila-Na-Gig, 'A woman with huge genitalia and a very large mouth, roaring in passion'.

From the start, Meabh was very headstrong and one who was used to getting her own way. Even though her dowry and marriage was such that she had exactly the same wealth as her husband, Ailill, she was not satisfied. She had an obsession with the sexual powers of Ailill and his bull and felt that they should not be greater that hers. This problem was exasperated by the fact that part of her dowry was several cows and heifers and Finnbhennach, the most fertile and beautiful white bull ever.

Now Finnbhennach was a bull with attitude, who, having charmed, bulled, butchered and bullied his way to becoming Laoghaire's leading lecherous light, of the loving, longing longhorns, was now a mere dowry filler for a woman, a fate worse than death.

When he arrived at Cruachán, he refused to have anything further to do with Meabh or her cows or heifers. But instead, with a sneering sidelong glance and a derisive snort, he put his tail on his back and galloped away to attach himself to Ailill's herd of cows

and heifers. When they saw this apparition coming in all his glowing white magnificence, there was a thunderous lowing welcome
from the cows and heifers while the bull in residence slunk away to
hide in the woods above Loughglynn.

Meabh flew into a rage and told Ailill that he could keep the
stupid bull and gave him advice as to what to do with him. This
advice was crude, crass, bestial, and physically impossible to carry
out. She swore that she would settle them both when she acquired
an even greater bull that would totally surpass and outdo Ailill and
Finnbhennach in every way.

On enquiry from her father, the king, Meabh heard of a champion brown bull, 'Donn Cuailnge', that was owned by a man
in Cooley, in the north east of the country, many miles from
Cruachán in Connaught. Meabh put an army together and with
her druids, headed for Cooley to buy, rent, borrow or steal the
brown bull from its owner, Dáire Mac Fiachna. After the long
journey through Meide, Dáire agreed to rent the bull to her for
three years. As the bull, Donn Cuailnge, had dominated Cooley
for the last three years he had to move on, as all the heifers were
his daughters. That is why Dáire was glad to rent the bull to one

who appeared honest and would pay the fee and return the beast in good condition. He also supplied them with food and drink and provided them with lodgings for the night. During the night he heard Meabh's soldiers boast that they would have taken the bull by force if necessary. This enraged Dáire and he hid the bull several miles away, on the other end of the peninsula.

Meabh spent days searching for the bull, during which time Dáire called on the great young warrior Cú Chulainn (Hound of Chulainn) for help. Now, eighteen-year-old Cú Chulainn, who was Ireland's greatest hurler, was also the most handsome man ever seen. So handsome was he, the men of Ulla requested the king to make a marriage match for him as all their wives, not to mention the young girls, were having fantasy fits about him. So brave was he as a boy, some years earlier, that when the fierce wolfhound belonging to Chulainn attacked him, he hit his sliotar (hurling ball) so hard with his ash hurl that it went down the throat of the charging hound and choked it. In compensation for the loss of the dog, the boy had to become the hound of Chulainn. Cú is the Irish for hound, hence the boy's name.

As ever, any young man who is a great hit with ladies found recruiting men friends more difficult, not to mention an army.

Cú Chulainn gathered an army eventually and blamed the God Macha for magically delaying him by putting him to sleep, but by then, Meabh had found the brown bull and was long gone. However, the bellowing of Donn Cuailnge gave away his location and Cú and his army followed.

When Meabh left she brought fifty heifers to coax and gratify Donn Cuailnge. After a day's journey, Meabh reached a small kingdom where lodgings were arranged for the night. By then, three of the heifers were in calf so she bartered them with the king for the night's lodging and three maiden heifers. The king agreed, as he was glad to get some progeny of the mighty brown bull. When he told his queen of the deal she put on her thinking cap. After a while she said, 'Why don't we sneak the brown bull out to all our heifers, just for the night? By morning, we might have several more in calf.' It was no sooner said than done and all Donn Cuailnge's dreams came true.

Early in the morning, when the king and his men went to bring the bull back before Meabh awoke, he and the heifers were on a distant hillside enjoying themselves. It took hours to bring them back and get them separated, as they resisted all the way. Who would want to abandon great sport? Donn Cuailnge was, surprise, surprise, so tired that they had to stay another night. This time Meabh left men all night guarding the bull.

When word of this delay reached Cú Chulainn he cut across country with his charioteer Láeg, hoping to intercept them at their next lodgings. Having travelled all day and all night, he arrived just as Meabh's party were leaving. The first of many skirmishes took place but because Cú and his men were so tired, Meabh and her people escaped with the bull.

By this time, Meabh had realised that Donn Cuailnge was a very valuable asset whose unborn progeny could be easily bartered and that he could be hired out for hours or days or weeks. In return, she could get food, lodging and, above all, fighting men. She decided that she could take her time, get richer, make more friends and fight off Cú Chulainn all at the same time. Not only that but she could make Cú look like a fool as she would take hundreds of unexpected detours all over Laigin and Midhe. One of the warriors she recruited was none other than Ferdiad, Cú Chulainn's best friend. Ferdiad assured her that he knew how to overcome Cú Chulainn as he had seen the method used by Cú to kill the many warriors who had fought him in single combat. It is best not to mention all of the rewards that were promised to Ferdiad, for, after all, Meabh was a married woman. The next day, Cú Chulainn and his charioteer Láeg confronted Meabh's cohort once again. Meabh demanded single combat between Cú Chulainn and her new champion Ferdiad.

She was sure that if she got rid of Cú Chulainn she would be able to return to Connaught at her own pace and unmolested. The battle between the two mighty warriors lasted several hours and the upper hand seemed to swing from one to the other. However, Cú Chulainn struck the final fatal stroke through the heart of Ferdiad.

Cú was so devastated at having killed his friend that he held him in his arms and wept bitterly. While Cú was mourning, Meabh fled.

Every time Cú and his army caught up there was war with many killed but Meabh and the bull continued this hazardous journey for seven years as Cú Chulainn was always blocking her way to Connaught. She travelled several times as far home as her outward journey on account of her determination to keep the bull despite the attacks, harassment and confrontation of the Ulla men.

And what about the resident bulls in all the herds that Meabh and Donn Cuailnge visited? Well, those resident bulls had a dilemma. Their testosterone demanded firstly that they defend their territory, secondly that they fight the newcomer but most of all, that they continue to service their heifers as requested. When they decided on option three and tried to jump on a heifer, they landed, not on the heifer, not the horns of a dilemma but alas, on the mighty sharp horns of Donn Cuailnge. They died in defence of their manhood.

Finally, when Meabh, Donn Cuailnge and her army crossed the Shannon at Athlone, Cú Chulainn and the Ullas made a last-ditch effort to capture the bull. They charged across the Shannon in pursuit and caught up just as Meabh and the Donn Cuailnge were being pulled through the dirty puddle at Baylough, half a mile west of the river. The puddle was there because, at that place, there was a dip in the esker and in times of high floods the Shannon overflow went through there, leaving a deep silted mucky pool. Cú Chulainn, because he was the fastest, arrived first, just in time to slice off Meabh's head while she was stuck. However, because he was the most honourable and valiant of all the warriors who ever lived, he could not strike a woman. Meabh and her brown bull were home, but not home and dry, as they were both very sorry-looking sights, covered in muck and barely able to stand.

By this time, Donn Cuailnge, the brown bull, and Finnbhennach, the white bull, were both twelve years old, had worn teeth, rheumatic pains and had lost most of their zest for sex or fight. When they finally met among the heifers at Cruahán they fought or jostled a little until tired and then went for a drink and a rest. That year the heifers went barren. After several months there was snow and in their last gentle fight, Finnbhennach slipped on the ice and died of the fall. Shortly after, Donn Cuailnge succumbed to the cold and died without siring a single Connaught calf.

What happened to Meabh? Did she return to Ailill? Was she buried on Inis Clothrann in Lough Ree where her sister Clothra lived? Was she buried on a mountain in Sligo? It would ruin many a great future rumour mill if I told. So I won't.

14

ONE CHRISTIAN ACCOUNT

Christianity was brought to Ireland by a man named Patrick. He and a man named Colmkill converted the people in the north of Roscommon while a holy woman named Bridget converted the southern half. This religion had a profound effect on everything in society and in every part of Roscommon and the whole country. It changed the people of Roscommon and all of Ireland forever. There were other Christians in Ireland before Patrick, but they did not know or understand the language, customs, or the system of living or spirit of the Irish people. They had remote monasteries and only had occasional converts. However, they brought Egyptian symbols, Celtic Crosses, images and specialised writing forms that outlasted their memory and influenced the great sacred writing and books of Ireland.

Patrick arrived across the Shannon at Drumboylan, in the parish of Ardcarne, and immediately started preaching, teaching, baptising and converting. A druid named Amwe decided to put a stop to this.

Amwe said to Patrick, 'I challenge any two of your new converts to a swimming duel in the River Shannon.' Patrick refused point blank, but the druid was insistent so Patrick said he would compete with the druid himself instead. The druid accepted as that was what he wanted all along and he was confident of drowning Patrick and so ending Christianity in Roscommon. It was arranged that at dawn the next day, Amwe and Patrick would dive into the river and there wrestle until one was drowned. The druid was a fast and nimble swimmer but Patrick was bigger and stronger. As they feigned, ducked and dived about each other a crowd gathered on the bank to cheer them on. When Amwe began to tire, Patrick at last managed to grab his two wrists and with a clever flip he had the druid with his hands behind his back. He could easily have held him under the water until he was drowned, but Patrick could not kill, even an evil druid. So he pulled him ashore and forced him to agree before the entire crowd that Patrick had won and they both agreed that was the end of it. Patrick then released the druid who ran away in shame and anger.

Amwe spent a long time licking his wounds. He had no physical wound but his pride was in bits. It could not be repaired. He could never show his face again. To be beaten and humiliated by anyone was intolerable, but to be overcome and put down by a meddling Christian was beyond bearing, beyond endurance and he just would not put up with it. He would get back at Patrick. He devised a plan.

He would drug two converts with a magic potion. He would send the very best incantations to the clouds. He was well aware that this type of incantation was dangerous and unpredictable but he didn't care. He did it anyway. It worked. The clouds came to a most unusual formation and Amwe incanted to the Gods of Clouds that this was to happen, in this place, every hundred years and that each time it happened, two Christians would be drowned. Immediately after, he met two new converts who foolishly agreed to a swimming duel, because they were drugged. All three dived into the Shannon. What the druid did not know was that neither of the converts could swim and when he approached them they grabbed him in total panic and hung on for dear life. Dear life it was, as all three soon sank and were drowned. At least two people have been drowned there every hundred years since, but had the movement of the clouds or the druid's evil magic anything to do with it? Who knows?

After this, Patrick, who was now more careful, travelled through mid and north Roscommon. A druid named Ono

Uí Briúin gave him a site at Imlock-Ónonn that soon became
known as Ail-Finn, Elphin. A church he built there was called
St Patrick's. Asicus, his smith, was the greatest artisan of his
time and he designed and made new altar-plate and metal book
shrines that were widely copied and written about. His artisan-
ship inspired many early Christian art, such as the Cross of Cong
and the Ardagh Chalice. This religion became so important that
a calendar dating from the birth of Jesus Christ was thereafter
used to measure time in the entire world. Not only that, but the
time before his birth is now referred as BC and the time after AD.

Soon after, there was a community of monks at Elphin where
the Abbot Bishop also resided. Centres of religion were built by
Patrick at Kilmore, Baslick, Strokestown, Fuerty, Oran, Tibohine,
Cloonshanville, and Kilnamanagh. He converted the daughters of
King Laoghaire, Eithne the Fair and Fidelma the Red, and baptised them in the well of Ogulla near Cruachán. This was then the
royal ceremonial and mystical centre of the capital of Connaught.

Patrick appointed Comgallen as Bishop of Boyle and St Maccan
followed him. It was then known as Áth Dá Larach. Ardcarn had its
own Bishop for a time but it was never a diocese. Patrick also founded
the first monasteries at Kilmore and Kilbarry. But is this true?

MYTH OR TRUTH?

One story says the monasteries were there already; that they had
been established by Coptic Christians who had come from Egypt.

St Mark went to Egypt at an early stage to try to establish
Christianity there. The Pharaoh power was waning but their religion was still strong. Their Sun God was round like the sun, and he
and the Pharaohs were always protected by the Cobra Semi-God.
St Mark could not get rid of those two symbols, so he adopted
them to the Cross. He put the Sun God as a big circle in the centre
of the cross, taking in the two arms and the upper and lower parts.

He had cobras hanging from several parts of the cross for protection. St Mark hoped that he or later generations would get rid of the Sun God and the Cobras but instead, the Coptics lost contact with Palestine and Rome and the cross with the snakes became the Christian symbol of Alexandria and Egypt. About the year 200, some of the Coptic Christians were being at least annoyed if not persecuted in Egypt and as they were monastic congregations, all they wanted was to live in peace, in quiet, remote places.

Ptolemy, an Egyptian sailor and cartographer, had visited, explored and made a recognisable map of Ireland 100 years before Christ. There were very experienced sailors in Alexandria in the following centuries and, of course, the Copts were among them. Some decided to sail away to find new peaceful places to live. As the Roman Empire covered all Europe except Ireland at that time, they arrived in Kerry. Having established a base and monastery there they did two things. Firstly, they sent word back home of the new land that they had found and encouraged others to come. Secondly, they slowly moved along the coast and up through the rivers, establishing a few monasteries here and there.

When Patrick encountered them in Roscommon he was pleased and terribly disappointed; pleased to meet other Christians but flabbergasted to see what they had done with the Cross of Jesus Christ. How could they? They must be serious heretics. However, when he got talking to them, he found that they were just as devout as he or any of his party. When he asked about the strange cross they were well able to explain, as they were well educated and had wonderful scriptoria and great scribes in their monasteries. Not only that but they had a considerable number converted and it would be difficult, if not impossible, for Patrick to claim that there were two Christian religions and even if he did, the others were there first and were well established. Compromise was called for.

After much debate between the two, Patrick agreed to keep the Sun God in the middle of the cross but they would rechristen it the Celtic cross and the Sun God would never be mentioned again. The Irish were delighted to have a cross named after them. In return for this concession, all agreed to get rid of the snakes. This didn't bother the Irish, as they never saw a snake anyway. However, it was agreed that Patrick would issue the decree and that all the Christians would help in its execution, to banish the snakes from Ireland. This was later interpreted as Patrick ushering the snakes into the sea with his croziers.

Patrick carried a crozier that depicted a shepherd's crook but it was different from the Coptic crozier, in that it had a flat head like a mallet. The reason for this was that in eastern areas the sheep were pets that followed their master and the crozier carried by the shepherd was for defending the sheep from attack from wolves. Therefore, it had a head that could deliver a good wallop. On the other hand, the

European, English and Irish sheep had plenty of grass and were independent, so the shepherd had to have a crooked crozier to catch them by the hind leg and pull them to him so that he could administer any needed attention. The mallet-head crozier is on the Cross of the Scriptures, that was erected in Clonmacnoise in the eighth century and is still there today.

Following the agreement about the Celtic cross and the snakes, both Christian evangelists worked together and they kept contact with Egypt for centuries using their skill, artistry, scholarship in the production of many wonderful books, ornaments and holy emblems. When the Copts were banished to the mountains in Egypt, the contact with Ireland ceased.

The new Christian religion declared that many of their leaders were saints soon enough after their death. This was a declaration that they had reached eternal life and salvation. They erected statues to many and named places after them. Some of those were St Colmcille, St Attracta of Killaraght, St Beoadh of Ardcarne, St Barry of Kilbarry and St Comán, who gave his name to the town of Roscommon. The main emblem of this religion was a cross with the dying Jesus Christ nailed to it. This cross was revered by all. It was taught that he died nailed to a cross after terrible scourging and torture at the hands of the Romans, encouraged by the Jews. But he rose again after three days and all who believe in him will live forever in eternal happiness.

In order to get general agreement from the druids, the Christians did not decry the cursing stones of the old religion, but etched crosses on them. This was done to nullify their magic properties and to brand them as Christian symbols. The druids did not realise the significance of this, but, in future years, it helped the Christians to diminish druidic practices and influences. They also persuaded the druids to accept the cross as a sacred symbol.

When St Patrick arrived in Oran and started baptising people at a well there, he was accosted by the local druid, Ami, who said that this was his holy well where he and his followers celebrated their

Lughnasa at the beginning of August. Patrick said that he regarded that as a great idea and that he and his followers would come too and join in the festivities. He added that his people would be celebrating the first Oran Pattern Day of Patrick. The druid did not realise that Patrick confidently expected that his religion would eventually take over the festival. Nor did he suspect that the new Christians would declare Patrick a saint and erect a statue to St Patrick almost immediately after his death. Nor did they know that the statue would be revered and honoured and that it would always be replaced, no matter how many times powerful enemies demolished it. On the other hand, Patrick did not realise that some of the Druidic practices would be there for more than another fifteen hundred years.

One day, Ami thought of a plan. He and his people had a magic stone in Fuerty called the La Téne Stone. It had circular inscriptions on it that the druids interpreted, making them messengers of the gods. He took Patrick there and explained that this magic stone, with its message from the gods, would preserve the Druidic beliefs and eventually banish the Christians from the country. Patrick blessed the stone, sprinkled it with holy water, looked Ami in the eye and asked if they could share it. Amazed, Ami agreed.

From there, Patrick went to Castlerea where he ordained Coavin to the priesthood and appointed him parish priest of Kilkeevan and abbot of the monastery that they built there. Naturally, they later called the church St Patrick's and the congregation were supposed to be subject the Bishop in Elphin.

There was a druid there named Ona who burst out laughing when he saw St Patrick baptising people in Longford Spring Well.

'What are you laughing at?' asked Patrick.

The druid replied, 'It was on the high ground yonder, that overlooks Castlerea, that our little people were once surrounded by a large force of Fir Bolgs. They were taken unawares and did not get a chance to produce their best magic and our Goddess Dana was busy in a far away part of the country. Our little folk

ducked and dodged all around the high ground but the Fir Bolgs were many and apart from those chasing among us they had a ring of mighty men all around the edge of the high ground. After a long day ducking, diving and dodging our little people were worn out and in danger of being captured. Just then, on a fairy blast our mini druidess, Sparkle, arrived. "All follow me," she said, and she led all the little people down a swallow hole and out of reach of the fierce Fir Bolgs.

'Were they all drowned? Not at all. Led by Sparkle, they emerged in these bubbling sparkling waters of Longford springs, laughing, splashing and playing. They imbued all who saw them with laughter and merriment and all who drank from the spring with their spirit forever. Now you are doing the same.'

Ona thought that this story would stop Patrick in his tracks. It didn't. Now he was very worried about Patrick's progress on his patch, so one evening at dusk he said to Patrick, 'Look west to our sacred mountain and see our great Lughnasa fire on its summit.' Patrick looked and, sure enough, there was a great fire on a distant conical mountain.

'Now,' said Ona, ' you may build a little wattle church here and imagine that you are making progress but our God will always oversee all Ireland from that, our wonderful holy mountain and neither you nor your weird religion will change that.'

'Perhaps your right,' said Patrick. Later, when it was coming to Samhain festival on 1 November, so Patrick declared that this festival would also be All Saints' Day, when Christians would remember and pray for their dead.

After this, Patrick made a plan; by this time next year he would be there again and the story of the Sacred Mountain would be different. The following June he climbed the Sacred Mountain in the far west. He brought with him forty oatcakes, six tin cans, two waterproof blankets, a stout stick and a warm woollen outfit. When he reached the summit he set about building a beehive hut with the flat stones there. When he had it finished, he spread one of the waterproof blankets over it, with the corners of the blankets settled on the stones so that they drained into the four tin cans set at the corners. By then it was evening so he wrapped the second waterproof blanket round the warm woollen outfit, crept into the little hut, prayed and slept peacefully. Next morning he ate just one of the oatcakes, drank some of the water collected in the cans and started his forty-day pilgrimage of prayer and fasting. He did the same every day but he also built a large cairn in the shape of a cross, blessed some of the water, sprinkled it all over the summit and declared this to be Ireland's Christian Holy Mountain. At the end of the forty days, Lughnasa and a great multitude bearing firewood, food, drink and sacrificial creatures arrived at the mountaintop.

'How are ye lads?' asked Patrick. 'You're welcome to the Patrick's Pattern and the Lughnasa Festival. But for a little oatcake, I've fasted here for the last forty days and I'm starving. Would ye have anything to eat?' As he was very thin and gaunt, like death warmed up, they gave him bread and butter and a leg of cold chicken. They were fascinated with him as they watched him eat like a man who had indeed fasted as he said. They were surprised to see Patrick there in the first place and were impressed with his beehive hut and amazed at his giant cross. Many of those who came were new

Christians who still celebrated Lughnasa, and when Patrick told them that this was also Pattern Sunday they lit the fire, cooked the food, made their sacrifices, opened the alcohol and all celebrated together.

Later, when Ona heard what happened and that Patrick had fasted for forty days and forty nights and built the huge cross, he became a Christian.

It's said that St Bridget evangelised South Roscommon, founding Christian sites at Drum, Clonown, Ballintubber, Kilbride, Dysart, Kilsellagh and Kilteevan. Her name is revered and remembered in many places, especially Brideswell. After the locals were converted to Christianity the well was called St Bridget's and it was claimed that any woman who drank from its waters and prayed to St Bridget would be helped with conception where necessary. The Christians also arranged a Pattern Sunday there to correspond with the feast of Lughnasa. This Pattern is still going strong and there are many stories of happy memories and outcomes from attendees.

There is a story that when St Bridget was in Kilteevan it was the Druidic feast of Bealtaine on 1 May and there were celebrations. Bridget joined in and claimed that the month of May was called after Mary, the Mother of Jesus, and that the day should therefore be called Lady Day in her honour. Of course, the day could also be called Bealtaine as well so there was no disagreement. When she arrived in Drum on 1 February, the day the feast of Imblooc occurred, Bridget asked that as she had just arrived on this day, if her name might be mentioned in connection with it. The druids were delighted as they had their own Goddess Brigit and thought they had converted her. However, after her death, the new Christians called the day 'Lá Fhéile Bríde', St Bridget's Day. Not only that, but the feast day occurs when winter is waning, buds are budding, lambs are leaping, songbirds are singing, and the world is awakening to new life, new hope and brighter days. This has inspired many bards, poets, writers, composers and musicians to ply their trade in praise of Bridget and 'Her day'.

But Bridget is remembered especially for her St Bridget's Cross that she fashioned from rushes. Because it is not made of wood it is a little off-centre, but it has hung in every home for her since her time. Indeed, this St Bridget's cross now hangs in houses throughout the world.

Soon after her time there was a tradition for children to call to neighbours singing and collecting for charity on St Bridget's day:

> Oh help us Saint Bridget for you are our kin
> And ask God to help us and keep us from sin.
> For you are our patron and never you fail?
> To make place in heaven for Éire and Gael.

> Ag teacht linn ar an mbothar trí Gorta Mhór
> Few people had oat cakes or bainne go leor.
> So inniu Lá Na Bríde will you kindly give
> A small morsel of food that others may live?

> As we came the road through the famine
> Few people had oat cakes or plenty of milk
> So today Bridget's Day will you kindly give
> A morsel of food that others might live.
>
> (Bilingual Famine Prayer and Begging Song)

There were also many monastic settlements on the islands in Lough Ree. Indeed, a descendant of the King of Tara, St Diarmaid, is said to have started monasteries on all the larger islands.

Those monastic people had to, or at least partly, obey the Brehon Laws that were there when they came. Those laws were based on an extended family or clan, with most things shared and everybody looked after. The monasteries, of course, brought writing, first in an eastern language, Latin, but later in the Irish language. This was another huge change for the people and gave them opportunities never before known.

By the time that St Patrick arrived in Ireland, the headquarters of Christianity was in Rome, from where it's Supreme Head, the Pope, governed. The bishops were supposed to be directed by the Pope but the Irish Christians initially followed much of the Druidic religion. Halfway through the sixth century there was extremely cold weather, causing famine and hardship. The druids were blamed for not foretelling this and lost credibility. This was a great help to the Christians but it was many years later before all traces of the druids were removed from Roscommon. Even the teller of this story is intrigued, inspired, mesmerised and driven by the Tuatha Dé Danann and their spirit.

After Christianity was established in Roscommon and Ireland it declined in much of Europe. By this time, the Irish monasteries were producing magnificent books, art and stone crosses. In later times of trouble some of those books were buried in bogs, where some, like the *Book of Kells*, were recovered centuries later. Some such books and artefacts may also be hidden in Roscommon bogs but have not been found yet, although parts of bog bodies, from an earlier time, were found near Lough Gara.

Following the decline of Christianity in Europe, Irish monks restored it in many places and many continental young men went there for training in our monasteries.

When some monasteries became rich and powerful, obedience to the words of Jesus Christ diminished and decadence prevailed. Then war between monasteries occurred and many lives were lost. Some of those problems were caused by noble families insisting on having members of their clan installed as abbots or bishops in charge. In some cases, there was even a right of succession established and, as a result, laymen became abbots.

At this stage, the Pope sent powerful emissaries to reform the Church in Roscommon, Lough Ree, Lough Cé and all Ireland. Some of those emissaries were not at all pleased with what they found and dictated strict rules for the future. They had totally opposite views on sex to Queen Meabh. She regretted that women could not be as clearly sexual as men, while those emissaries wanted sex restricted even among married people. It was never quite clear how those directions could be implemented.

The Roscommon people, and monasteries in general, agreed wholeheartedly to obey their strict rules, but many lapsed when the emissaries left, not really having wholeheartedly agreed in the first place.

Indeed, many genuinely devout Roscommon and Irish mission-aries went all over the world for millennia, preaching and teaching Christianity and converting whole nations. No doubt the magical Irish spirit of the Tuatha Dé Danann was most useful to them. It created their friendliness, good humour and daring, gift of the gab, music poetry and writing, while their holiness came from Jesus Christ.

St Patrick could never have foreseen that 1,500 years after his time, all over the world, rivers, cities, statues and mountains would be turned green in his honour and he would be one of the most widely remembered saints in the world.

'There are more people in various parts of the world claiming to be Irish and wearing green, than there was in the whole world in your time. You can believe it Patrick.'

15

St Ciaran of Clonmasnoise & Fr Pat Whitney of Drumboylan

St Ciaran was from Fuerty in Roscommon. As a child, he lived near the La Téne stone. He was Roscommon's first Christian missionary. He grew up herding cows for his father, Beoit, who was a carpenter. Like most Irish people he was descended from the Tuatha Dé Danann people, with the blood of poets, bards, music makers and historians running through his veins. He was baptised a Christian by Deacon Justus, who also taught him a great many things. From an early age, he was a very devout Christian and was known as 'the righteous one'. He had a great affinity with animals, wild and tame, and mostly, they did his bidding.

He went to the monastery at Clonard, that was headed by St Finnian, for education. He became the most learned monk there and taught the daughter of the King of Cuala in his spare time. Among his schoolmates was Columcille, who later became the famous St Columcille of Iona in Scotland. Others there were St Senan of Scattery Island, St Kevin of Glendalough and St Enda of the Aran Islands. It was said later that Ireland's Twelve Apostles were all there at that time.

When he was going to Clonard, he brought a cow as a present for the abbot. The calf belonging to the cow followed, but when Ciaran drew a line in the dust and ordered the calf not to cross it, the calf obeyed and went back to the farm. On arrival at the monastery the cow produced enough milk to provide the entire monastery with milk, butter and cheese and had plenty left for the poor. After Clonard, he spent time in the monastery on Inishmore of the Aran Islands.

During his time there with St Enda, they both had a vision of a great tree on the bank of a river, and Enda told Ciaran, 'God is asking you to go and found a monastery there and multitudes will benefit from it and be drawn to God. The great tree represents you who will be an inspiration and a calling to piety to all Ireland for all time.'

Soon after this occurrence, Ciaran went for a time to Scattery Island before returning to his midlands brothers at Isel. He was not very welcome there and so he moved to Hare Island in lower Lough Ree. During the three years he spent there, he was joined by eight monks who marvelled at his piety and miracles.

The nine of them set off down the Shannon, through the rapids in Athlone and on south, where snow and strong winds forced them ashore on the Roscommon side of the river at Clonown. Here they were taken in, dried out, well fed and put up for several days and nights until the weather improved. As they took their leave, Ciaran blessed Clonown for their generosity and kindness and foretold that they would always have plenty of milk and butter and that they will never go hungry.

Thirteen hundred years later, when the Great Famine came to the parish of Clonown, St Peter's and Drum, the population of Drum and St Peter's were halved by hunger, disease and emi-gration, but due to Ciaran's blessing, the Clonown population remained the same throughout this terrible time.

By the end of January Ciaran and his group had arrived at a remote grassy hillside, north of the Clonascra hills. Ciaran said, 'Here we will stay, for many souls will go to heaven hence. There will be a visit from God and from men forever at this place.' This will later be taken by many to mean that all buried here will have eternal salvation.

On 23 January 544, Ciaran laid the foundation stone of his monastic school at Clonmacnoise. By the month of May they had completed it, watched by Diarmait, son of Cerball, later High

King of Ireland. Cerball promised Ciaran extensive lands to support his monastery and produce to feed its pupils.

Alas, in September a plague ravaged the country killing many, including our own saintly Ciaran. He will forever be remembered for his goodness while his faults were buried with him. As St Ciaran lay dying he requested the novice who was looking after him to go at the first opportunity and establish a monastery at his beloved Clonown. This was done soon after.

The school and monastery went on to greatness, educating holy men from all parts of Ireland as well as many from several European countries. One reason why it was successful was that successive abbots came from different provinces throughout Ireland and were always supported by the bishops. As this monastery consisted of many wattle and clay houses, thatched with reeds from the Shannon, it had many serious outbreaks of fire but always recovers quickly. Plague returned to the monastery again in the seventh century and killed many students and monks. By then it was the greatest centre of learning in all Europe. They had a wonderful scriptorium where very skilled and dedicated monks produced great manuscripts. This was the time that Ireland became known as the Island of Saints and Scholars.

Many High Kings of Ireland and many Kings of Connaught were buried at the monastery, as well as many ordinary people from both sides of the Shannon. The people from the Roscommon side brought their dead there by boat and hazardous though those journeys were, there were few mishaps and not a single corpse was lost in the river. For a short few years there was a bridge across the Shannon at this point, built by the O'Conor Kings, but warring factions pulled it down.

Clonmacnoise was plundered many times by various Irish factions but always recovered quickly. In the ninth and tenth centuries the Vikings came up the Shannon from Limerick and pillaged the monastery many times. But, after their time, the monastery recovered and prospered until the sixteenth century, when the English

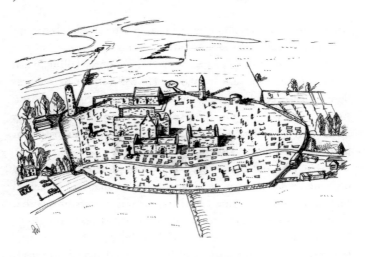

soldiers from Athlone finally destroyed it and closed it down permanently. The Protestants claimed it as their own and used one of the churches for their services. However, it was always a holy place to the Catholics and they eventually reclaimed it.

But the spirit of the magic people was always there. Shortly before it was finally sacked, a monk named Odo Malone fashioned a great ornamental stone archway around the door on the north side of the church. The arch looked like a series of half pipes going from the ground, right up and over the top and coming down the other side making groves all the way. Of course this was done for the honour of God and to impress all who come to this church.

When the soldiers burnt the church, the roof, the door and all the timbers were destroyed but the arch and walls survived. In later times, Catholics called this place Seven Churches and held patterns there every year. As there were no priests, the patterns became social occasions where young people met just for the craic. One day, a girl whispered into one of the groves and her friend on the other side of the arch heard her perfectly. But when she spoke into the grove, the loud words did not carry – only whispers worked. Soon, everybody present tried the whispering and it was found that only those with their ears close to the other could hear. While a certain girl had her ear to the arch, listening, a secret admirer whispered 'Will you marry me?' When she turned around blushing, she was well pleased with her smiling admirer and answered 'Yes'. Thereafter this became the proposing capital of a wide area. The spirit of the Tuatha Dé Danann came with Ciaran from Roscommon and survived through prayer, piety, plague, pestilence, peace and wayward warring warriors.

Maybe it was fate, maybe it was divine intervention or maybe was just coincidence, but P.J. Whitney was born in Drumboylan in 1894. This was the same place where St Patrick first set foot in Roscommon more than 1,400 years before.

St Patrick first came to Ireland as a slave who was sold to a pig farmer in Northern Ireland. He was a devout sixteen-year-old Christian at this time and Ireland was mostly a pagan country. For six years he prayed night and day to his Christian God. But, as he prayed, the spirit of our little people penetrated his mind. Finally, his prayers were answered and a vision told him to walk a hundred miles south where a boat was waiting to take him home. He felt elated to be escaping his captors, his owner and the cold damp country to which those wild men had taken him in the first place. Still being a devout man he studied and became a priest with the intention of having a quiet, holy and civilized life. But our Tuatha Dé Danann little people were in his mind and every night in his dreams, they called him back to

the west of Ireland. He was the first of many foreigners who came to change us but who became more Irish than the Irish themselves. When he told his superiors of his recurrent dream they ordained him bishop and advised him to return to Ireland, which he did.

As he had learned the language during his slave years, he was able to communicate and the Irish were receptive to his new religion. He established his beliefs among the kings around Tara in order to give himself free passage to the west from where the little people were calling. When he crossed the Shannon at Drumboylan, his heart lurched with anticipation and he gave a great sigh. The breath from this sigh rode on a fairy blast supplied by our people and this fairy blast remained around Roscommon for a very long time. As a child, St Ciaran was inspired by it, as was St Coman and many others. But Drumboylan was always home to this particular fairy blast, as it was watching out for a child of the distant future.

Now what had this to do with Pat Whitney? He, like St Ciaran before him, had met the fairy blast and he was imbued with a great religious zeal. He was ordained a priest for the Diocese of Ardagh in 1920 but like St Patrick before him he never ministered where he originally intended. One Bishop Shanahan CSSP, who was a bishop in Nigeria, appealed for help from Irish young priests. Fr P.J. was the first young priest to go with Fr Thomas Ronayne, who was seven years his senior. Ten more young priests joined them soon after.

Fr P.J. decided to form a new missionary order. Naturally it was called St Patrick's Missionary Society. A merchant named John Hughes gave them over 200 acres of land in Kiltegan, Co. Wicklow. That's why they are sometimes called the Kiltegan Fathers.

The first three members were: Fr P.J. Whitney, who was appointed Superior General, his cousin, Fr Patrick Francis Whitney, who had worked in Nigeria, and Fr Francis Hickey, a priest who spent some time in Australia. They took the oath of membership on St Patrick's Day, 1932, the day that Ireland was celebrating the 1,500th anniversary of the coming of St Patrick to Ireland.

This society was a great success and, in the first year, ten more young men came to Kiltegan. This number increased annually and like Clonmacnoise before it, there were generous benefactors from all over Ireland and the students helped in every way with its development. In due course there were 400 priests from this order preaching, teaching and baptising in Nigeria, Kenya, Malawi, Zambia, Zimbabwe, Cameroon, Grenada, Republic of South Sudan, South Africa, Brazil and West Indies. In eighty years they have influenced nearly as many people as St Ciaran.

When the Irish Church waned and fewer were becoming priests, they were replaced in abundance by indigenous priests from the countries that they had evangelised. Some have even come to work in Ireland. So, like Ciaran before him, our own Fr P.J. Whitney from Roscommon will be remembered forever.

16

A STORY ABOUT
RATHRA FORT

In early Christian times, the Byrne family were out hunting. When they came to the Hill of Rathra, they stopped their horses to access the possible position and likely flight path of their intended prey. Their hopes were high that day, as there was a strong west wind on their faces as they looked across the four miles of lowlands of scrub, shrubs, swamp and sedge to the River Suck. The dogs were under control but were restless as the scent of deer and wild pig assailed their nostrils. The wild creatures were upwind, and they could neither scent nor hear the hunters.

Brian and Fin Byrne and Ono OG, sent the two eighteen-year-olds, Ferdi and Pat, on a circular mile-wide beating tour so that they could get the far side of some deer or pig, where they would blow horns and frighten the prey in the direction of the men, spears and dogs. It was a typical west-of-Ireland day with black clouds, sunshine, rainbows and wind playing games in the sky. Then it happened – Ferdi was in a rainbow. It lit up his hair and clothes in a magical colourful way. Ono OG cried out, 'At last I have one.' He got sideways worried glances.

While all were Christians, Ona OG, who was now elderly, was descended from a family of Filads, druids who passed on their beliefs and magic verbally to future generations. Ona OG knew that anyone who reached the end of the rainbow would find a crock of gold there and restore the ancient religion. Young Ferdi was the man. The hunt continued successfully and no more was said.

About this time there was a family row among the O'Donnell Clan in the north. The family consisted of Fionn, the chief, his wife, Aoife and his sons, Fionn Oge and Black Hugh. Aoife had immediately called Hugh black when he was born with a mop of black hair. His father named him after his uncle. Nobody outside the family quite knew what the row was about but the result was that Black Hugh, the second son, was given his share of the estate and banished from Ulster forever. This was serious stuff. He came south with a considerable number of men, horses, goods and chattels including many bartering goods in iron, gold, copper, bronze and valuable stones. He tried his luck in Sligo but was always ushered on until he passed Lough Gara, where he heard of the hill of Ratha with its lush pastures. He arrived there, made an immediate deal for the hill and its surrounds and set up his tent. Night came and so did the wolves. Then he knew why he got such a good deal.

After a hard night fighting the wild creatures, the next day all set to work building a ring fort. Because of his wealth, he was able to recruit many locals. After strong exhortations from Ono OG, Ferdi was among them.

'Go there,' said Ono OG, 'eat all you're able, drink only water, keep your ears open and your mouth shut and work as if it was your own and one day it will be.'

The clay was easy to handle, with no stones, and, in a short time, they had an ark that was easier defended by night. Eventually they got the huge inner ring completed. It seemed that the wolves had sent messages to far-away friends to come and help, because the nightly attacks continued and it took many men and hounds to man the clay ring. There was nothing for it but to build another ring outside and put a moat in the middle.

Over time this was done, and to make the canal in the middle waterproof, geese and ducks were fed in the bottom of it, and as their oily droppings were mixed with the clay and rain and padded solid by the webbed feet, it became watertight and filled up. The wild creatures gave up. Neighbouring clans took up where they left

off. Another outer ring and second canal had to be put in place. The only problem was that in fine weather the water in the canals dropped low and became dirty and poisonous to man and beast. The nearest water was a mile away at the bottom of the hill.

Ono OG watched all this activity with growing concern as the fort was over Ferdi's crock of gold, and, above all, he did not want to break his promise. He was getting old and in spite of getting him working in the fort, his efforts to influence and tutor Ferdi were continually being thwarted by his parents and Peter, the Abbot of Kilkeevan.

By the time Ferdi was twenty-five years old he was head manager in the fort and had fallen in love with the beautiful Fidelma Hanley. As ever, there were problems. Ferdi was not the heir apparent, only a workman, and Fidelma and her family were deemed to be inferior, partly because of her pedigree and parentage, but mostly because of her tiny dowry and her having no farm or house where Ferdi could have hung up his hat.

Double luck struck for Ono OG. Ever since Black Hugh had taken over what he considered his pot of gold, Ono OG was determined to find out everything about this grabbing stranger. The travelling bards were sympathetic to Ono OG and his ancient beliefs. Finea was one such bard and he had just returned from the north with news about the O'Donnell that he relayed to Ono OG. Black Hugh had a much more serious falling out with his father, Fionn, and his brother, Fionn Oge, than locals thought. Some said it went back a generation to when Fionn and his brother Red Hugh had a row about Mary O'Neill on the shore of Lough Neagh. Mary's father tried to separate them but Red Hugh stabbed him before the O'Neill sons cut him down. Fionn escaped with his life, but the romance was over. He never forgot Mary and always blamed Red Hugh and blamed himself for thinking bad of the dead. His oldest son was a gentleman like himself but Black Hugh was difficult from the start. His mother should never have called him Black and he should have avoided the name Hugh. Wasn't one unfortunate Hugh enough in any family? Maybe that was why he dealt very harshly with him when he banished him from the province.

Shortly after Black Hugh left, things started to go wrong. Several cows and sheep aborted prematurely that year and his prize bull was drowned. The bad luck had only started, though, as in June, Fionn fell from his horse while hunting and did not awake for two days. Worse still, when he did waken, he seemed to have lost his zest for life. He lost interest in girls, drinking, hunting and all leisure activity. Every year he got worse and worse and eventually he had started talking to trees. He said they were decent creatures that never answered back, only sighed softly to his suffering soul. His father was heartbroken and felt he was being punished by God for his treatment of Black Hugh and his uncle before him. He had no other son and he wished Black Hugh were home again to take over from him and carry on his name. However, he knew little of Black Hugh, how he was getting on or even his whereabouts.

Ono OG hatched a plan.

He gave the bard half his gold and instructed him to go back North and tell Fionn senior that he would bring him back his lost son, if he had an invitation and a sizable reward for the bard. Fionn thought of the biblical story of the prodigal son and he wept as he saw the hand of God in the plan. He readily agreed and gave the bard considerable wealth and his gold ring, with instructions that it was to be given to his son Hugh – he would never call him Black Hugh again. Then, he said, 'Hugh will not believe you and if he thinks that you stole the ring or murdered me to get it, he will surely kill you. I will give you a few bits of secret information about the family that you must relate to none but Hugh.'

Finea, the Bard never said that he was working for another. On his return, he gave half of what he got to Ono OG. He also gave Ono OG back his original inducement, the ring and the family secrets.

Ono OG went to work. Firstly, he went to Ferdi and promised him that he would get him ownership of all of Rathra together with the fort and his pot of gold. Then he could marry the beautiful Fidelma and live in blissful happiness ever after. In return, Ono OG wanted a high tower that could be seen for miles built in the middle of the fort. On top of this tower he wanted a stone bust of Butch, the famous hound of the ancient religion. Ferdi thought of Fidelma, he seldom thought of anything else. Now this kind old man was offering him everything he had ever dreamed of and much more. He could have his heart's desire, he could be lord of the best fort in the country, and he would do it. Then a terrible thought came to him, 'What about Abbot Peter of Kilkeevan?' He would go mad. He would banish him to hell. He would send for Bishop Asicus of Elphin. They would expel him from the Christian Church altogether. His family would be disgraced. All belonging to him would be disgraced. But wait, he would have Fidelma, the fort, the pot of gold and glorious embracing happiness in this life. He would do it.

'You promise to keep your word about the tower and our ancient wolfhound?' said Ono OG.

'I do,' said Ferdi.

Ono OG set off to see Hugh O'Donnell at the fort. 'It grieves me to see one of royal blood like you, toiling here in the west, when your rightful place is as leader of Ireland's greatest clan in glorious Ulster, where the mountains are majestic, the lakes glittering, the men brave, the girls beautiful and the plains rich in milk and honey.'

'My good wife and I are indeed pining for home but we have been banished forever from Ulster and now our young sons will never see it,' said Hugh.

'If I could convince your father to bring you back and to give you all his lands and titles, what would you do for me?'

'But that is totally impossible, my father is not a man to change his mind, nor am I and the great gulf between us is impossible to bridge.'

'I assure you I can do as I say and, to prove my credentials, I can tell you that your brother Fionn is suffering from the malady and will never marry or produce an heir.'

'How would an old man like you know such things?' said Hugh.

'I have my ways, and not only do I know,' said Ono OG, 'but I can prove that I had contact with your father and that he would like reconciliation with you.'

'Prove it,' said Hugh.

Ono OG showed him the ring.

'You are either the greatest rogue that God ever created or you are the cleverest man alive, for my father would not part with his ring while there was a single breath left in his body. You will need more proof or you will not leave this fort alive.'

'Where and how did your uncle Red Hugh die?' said Ono OG.

'You tell me or you die,' said Hugh.

'He died on the shore of Lough Neagh, cut down by the O'Neills after he had murdered their father.'

'One last question,' said Black Hugh, 'who named me?'

'Your mother the first part and your father the second part,' came the reply.

'I have to agree that you're good, you're very good but if I do believe you, what is it you want and what's in for you?'

'I want you to appoint your manager Ferdi to look after your business here and go north with your family to meet your father.

If what I say is true you will have extensive lands and forts in your own Ulster and you will send word that Ferdi can keep Rathra. If not, you can return, kill me and Ferdi and reclaim your three-ring-fort here.' After some thought and discussions with his family, Hugh accepted the offer on condition that Ono OG told no one of the deal until word came back. A few days later, when he had his entourage assembled he set out for Ulster, with Finea, the bard, leading them out with the music of his lyre.

As soon as they were gone, Ferdi said to Ono OG, 'Now I will dig for the gold if you show me the exact position as with all the digging and building I'm not sure where to dig and anyway, it was you and not I who saw me in the rainbow.' Ono OG thought for a moment, he quickly realised that he had another advantage. How would he use it?

'There are two reasons why you should not dig now. The first is that Hugh may change his mind and return any time and then we would all be in trouble. The second reason is that you cannot dig for gold on another man's property. Just wait a few weeks for Finea to return with word that Hugh has taken over his father's estate, that he is not coming back and then I will keep my promise to you that one day you would own it all.' Ferdi still demanded to be shown the exact spot where the gold was to be found and so Ono OG walked over and marked the spot with his heel, as he wanted to keep Ferdi quiet for the last few days.

A month later, Finea returned with the great news that Hugh was not coming back and that Ferdi was now the owner of Rathra. He immediately started to dig for the gold. After only going down a few feet he came upon a gushing spring well that bubbled up and flowed down the hill. Ferdi turned to Ono OG, 'Where is the gold?' he asked.

'That's it, flowing past your feet and it's in the eyes of the beautiful Fidelma standing beside you and the love you share and its in all the property you now own, no metal could ever match that.' Ferdi and Fidelma knew that he was right and that they had all they needed.

'Now,' said Ono OG, 'we will build the tower as arranged.' Ferdi was fearful of the abbot and the bishop, but, as he was a man of honour, he kept his bargain and built the tower that could be seen for miles. Not only that, but it was built with four three-foot-thick oak trunks. They were sunk in the ground, narrow end down, with the thicker, squared ends meeting at the top to make a nine-foot square platform. To hold the trunks together he had a six-inch square grove cut into the platform, across all the tree trunks. This grove tapered out wider towards the edges and into this he dropped a cross with widening arms to match the tapered grove. When the cross was hammered in tightly, the whole structure was very solid and Ferdi hoped that the cross would also undo the influence of the idolatrous dog and save him from eternal damnation.

Ono OG located a large stone a quarter of a ton weight and commissioned a sculptor to fashion the bust of the ancient Irish wolfhound, Butch. With considerable pomp and ceremony this was placed on top of the tower and indeed, it could be seen for miles. To Ferdi's relief and surprise there was not a word, good, bad, or indifferent from priest, abbot or bishop. Those wise men had figured rightly that the ancient religion was almost completely forgotten and that the old man Ono OG was not long for this world. They were right. Ono OG died before the year was out and soon the tower and the sacred hound was being called Ferdi's Folly. However, Ferdi was a man of his word and the tower and dog remained throughout his lifetime. By then, Ferdi's Folly was a land mark and it enhanced the appearance of the fort.

Several generations later, when the timbers finally rotted, the heavy bust fell through and lay among the rubble. No sooner did this happen, than the spring well dried up and without fresh water, many contracted disease and the fort had to be abandoned.

Today, the remains of the long-abandoned fort are still there, together with the bust of Butch so weathered that few people now realise what it is.

17

STORIES OF
DIFFERING O'KELLYS

There was a Kingdom called Uí Máine in the south of Roscommon and it stretched further south along the Shannon. The O'Kellys were kings there, and they had powerful under lords, the O'Naughtains (Naughtens) and O'Fallúins (Fallons). At one time or another, this kingdom included all of the area between the Shannon and the Suck from Roscommon town south. It also took in large parts of Galway and extended as far south as Clare. Sometimes it included most of Lough Ree and its islands. There were many Kings of Uí Maine and they were supportive of Connaught Kings, rather than rivals, although the odd murderous war did break out. This region was called after Máine Mór who set up the kingdom in the first place by subduing all around him.

The O'Kelly's had many other legends of great, brave and clever things done by or to their ancestors, and one such legend concerned Brian Boru when he was endeavouring to become of High King of Ireland.

In the late tenth century, Brian Boru came to power in Clare and soon took over all of Munster, defeating Viking and Irish opposition as he went. He then came up the Shannon to attack the Connaught O'Conor and Malachi of Leinster but the combined forces of both blocked him just above Shannonbridge where they had a wall built across the river to stop the boats. At this time The O'Kellys were Kings of Uí Maine, an area that stretched along the Shannon from Lanesboro to the top of Lough Derg.

Brian Boru had brainwave. He was well aware of the Irish love of sport, feasting, drink and the craic. Instead of fighting, he decided to host a big party for the O'Kellys, on the west side of the river at Shannonbridge. His cooks had bullocks, sheep and pigs turning on the spit and drink to beat the band with the fairies cheering them on. The feast lasted for a week and, by then, Brian Boru and the O'Kelly were best buddies and, amid much back-slapping and drinking to each other's health, they helped each other clear the wall out of the river. Brian then brought his boats as far as Athlone. He then sent an emissary to ask Malachi to talks. Malachi set up camp on the island 'Sing Two Birds'. Brian left his boats in Killumper and walked with his men through the bushy callows of Clonburn to arrive on the island. There, on that day, the fate of Ireland and the Vikings was decided. Malachi agreed to divide Ireland half-and-half with Brian. After more wining and dining, on different occasions, Malachi finally agreed to Brian Boru becoming High King of Ireland. A few years later, this led to the defeat of the Vikings at Clontarf.

As a result of the friendship forged between Brian Boru and the O'Kellys at Shannonbridge, the latter sent a large army to assist Brian Boru at the Battle of Clontarf. When the O'Kelly king's son was injured and dying on the beach there, a Viking approached him to finish him off and dismember his body, as that was the done thing at this time. Just as he approached the dying man, an enfield, a type of hound, emerged from beneath the sea waves and stood guard over the dying O'Kelly. This gave an opportunity for another O'Kelly to cut down the Viking. The hound then disappeared but one of those who saw him made an image of him from memory and so he appears on the O'Kelly Coat of Arms forever. The enfield appeared for a minute but he lives forever.

Many years later, another O'Kelly, William Boy, heard this legend and decided to use the knowledge gained for his own ben-efit. It was a custom at his time for the various kings to invite the local bards, poets, harpists, wizards, singers and entertainers to their castles for Christmas and other festivals.

So it was that, in 1351, King William Boy O'Kelly decided to have the greatest Fleadh Ceoil (music feast) of all time at his castle in Galey, in the parish of Knockcrockery. He invited all the bards, poets, singers, harpists, wizards, cartoonists, jumping jacks and even common cairógs. Cairóg also meant tricksters and some of them came in disguise dressed as other people, creatures, or even dressed as women. Some smart people at this festival were surprised to see so many and remarked '*Aithnionn cairóg, cairóg eile*'. The remark generally means that one shyster recognises another shyster, and it was remembered, repeated and recorded as an old Irish saying that would be used for hundreds of years. Indeed, it became the bane of schoolchildren for generations.

King William's purpose was threefold. Firstly, he invited all the entertainers in Ireland and Scotland, depriving all others of their service. Secondly he and his friends really had the ball of all balls and, thirdly, he created the everlasting Fáilte Uí Cheallaigh phrase: The Welcome of the O'Kellys, and it became an even greater welcome than Cead Mile Fáilte (a hundred thousand welcomes).

This enterprise was so big that it had to be planned a year in advance and it took a hundred men to put everything in place. There were messengers sent throughout Ireland and Scotland with attractive invitations. The offer included board, lodgings, drink and entertainment all over Christmas, into the New Year and on to St Bridget's Day (1 February). Invitees were also told that they would get presents for the road, ample to bring them comfortably back to their home parts or to their next port of call. This final inducement convinced all to come.

Then several villages of little huts were built for the visitors. Those wattle huts had to be substantially daubed with waterproof clay to keep out rain and winter weather. The inside walls were hung with cow hides for heat retention. They were thatched with tons of reeds harvested from the Shannon. Each village housed different type of artists. In this way, artists were able to have joint sessions and learn all the latest from other parts.

In order to provide fresh meat and fish for all the visitors, King William had 300 wicker cleaves made; large baskets big enough to hold four-quarters of a butchered heifer or bull. Two hundred beef carcasses were stored in this way, slung from rafts beneath the cold waters of Lough Ree. The baskets were sealed in watertight skins to be recovered as necessary. The other hundred baskets that had looser woven wicker each contained six live salmon that could also be recovered when needed. They too were held below water and fed daily from above. A granary was built some distance away where large quantities of corn were stored. All those goods were received in taxes or donations from various parts of the kingdom and subservient kingdoms by way of tribute.

And the drink! Well, there were barrels and barrels of mead; twenty opened all the time so that nobody would have to far to go for a refill. And did they refill! There was more refilling, glass tipping and calling 'sláinte' than was ever known in Roscommon before. Now the poitin whiskey was in hundreds of two-gallon earthenware jars and there was more than ample for all. Indeed, the rarest thing at this Fleadh Coiel was a sober person.

Finally, the mighty Fleadh Ceoil, 'The musical party that was the mother of all musical parties', got into full swing and lasted for a full month. There were harps, horns, lutes, lyres, tin whistles, brass whistles, wood whistles, trumpets, trombones, drums, bellows and bodhráns to beat the band. And the dancing! Sure they were dancing up the walls and down the other side.

So satisfied and gratified were all present, that King William did indeed achieve all his aims and established *Fáilte Uí Cheallaigh* as the best of all Irish greetings. He also had annoyed the other rulers who had to make do with second-rate entertainment and his ball is the ball that will be remembered forever. From this time forward, people who visited Galey Bay and its environs often reported amorous or loving feelings they had while there and some even broke into song or composed and recited poems about those feelings, not to mention other things they may have done.

DEVIOUS DEVIL O'KELLY

Some say it was Roscommon Castle, some say it was another Roscommon castle, while others say it was Killer Bingham Castle in Tulsk, but it was definitely Devious Devil O'Kelly. He was not the owner but a minion of the owner who had power over the staff and tenants. His use of this power was more tyrannical than all the other tyrannies of all of the other tyrants in Roscommon, and there were many.

As most of the staff and all of the tenants were very poorly dressed and fed, it was felt inappropriate that any visitors should have to encounter such wretches. Therefore, there was an underground passage from the farmyard to the castle cellar for those underlings to come to work or pay rent or tithes. Here, they met Devious Devil who dealt with them on behalf of his overlord. He always charged a bit over the odds, giving half to his overlord and pocketing the rest for himself. In this way, he ingratiated himself with the master and, at the same time, covered his tracks. If it ever reached the master's ears that he was overcharging, the master would assume that he had got the entire overcharge and would feel happy that Devious Devil had handled the situation.

The master, when riding round his estate, would always be on the lookout for a pretty young virgin. Whenever he saw one, he would order that she be taken to his castle, washed, suitably dressed and taken to his bedroom for his pleasure. Whenever he tired of her, he would marry her off to a tenant farmer, who would be rewarded with another acre or two of land that would be taken from another tenant of Devious Devil's choosing. If this resulted in hunger, hardship or even starvation for the dispossessed, it only added to Devious Devil's power and effectiveness as the master's lackey. Devious could now instil fear all around and blame the master, but everyone knew the final, fateful, or fatal decision was his. He had many enemies and, if thoughts could kill, he would not last long. But alas, thoughts cannot kill.

The old cook had learned this the hard way. When Devious Devil had her only remaining son and his heavily pregnant wife evicted because of a perceived slight, they resisted the soldiers. The daughter and the unborn grandchild were shot and her son hanged. Dead or alive, widow's curses are dangerous.

As time went by, Devious Devil got wealthier, more arrogant and more unbearable. He got to thinking that he was nearly as good as the master and that he should be entitled to the first night with one of the young peasant girls. He was well aware that if the master ever got wind of this, his last day would surely have come. However, when an overly ambitious man who feels he has arrived gets amorous notions about a helpless female, passion may over-rule common sense. He hatched a plan that suited his name.

Sixteen-year-old Mary Jones was an auburn-haired beauty, with magnificent sea blue eyes, the melodious voice of an angel and the majestic bearing of a queen. When Devious Devil saw her he was immediately smitten. He greatly feared the master, but the bad thoughts that had been feeding his mind, his dreams and his passion were now insistent on gratification. Did he wrestle with his conscience? Did he argue with his conscience? You must be joking: he didn't have a conscience. No, he argued with himself. This is a chance not to be missed, but the master will murder me. Are you a man or a mouse? I have as good courage as any man. Well, use it then. But how? You promised me in your dreams. They were dreams this is the light of day. You're only a coward with no balls. Do you hear whose talking balls? You are persistent, you will give me no peace; I will make a plan.

Devious Devil had his own room, in an annex a half flight above the cellar. How could he get Mary here? The master was away. He would just call to her house before dawn the next morning, say the master sent him for Mary and just carry her off. He would bring her by the tunnel before anyone was awake and sneak her up to his room. It was a foolproof plan, he was a genius, and nothing could go wrong.

What Devious didn't know was that Big Tom Ward from a neighbouring parish had also met the beautiful Mary a few months back and that he too was smitten. Unlike the sneaky Devious Devil, Big Tom had approached the girl, smiled at her, and complimented her on her hair, grace and beguiling smile. She reciprocated and from then they met twice weekly. Now, Big Tom was a famous, fierce, faction fighter even though he was only twenty-years-old. Yet this shillelagh-wielding, man-scattering giant was as gentle as the morning gossamer in Mary's arms. Even her longing for intimacy was lovingly and gently declined for the sake of her honour.

When Devious Devil called to Mary's house on his horse and took her before daylight, her father, who knew that the master was away, sent young Paddy running to tell Big Tom. When Devious Devil reached the tunnel he dismounted and quickly overpowered Mary, tying her hands behind her back and gagging her mouth lest she cry out. When she refused to walk he picked her up and carried her down the tunnel to the cellar. Then he escaped up the half stairs to his den, unseen but not quiet. The old cook was a poor sleeper. As he tried to ravish poor Mary she resisted with such ferocity that the attempted lovemaking turned into a prolonged life and death struggle, during which she bit off the top of his nose and seriously damaged his manhood with her knees. Alas, it was poor Mary who lost the battle against the tightening fingers on her throat. She died fighting to the finish with her virtue intact.

Devious Devil was standing over her in a dastardly stupor when Big Tom arrived in the cellar. The old cook pointed to the half stairs. Big Tom was in the den with one bound. He laid Devious Devil low with a mighty blow and ran to his dead Mary. The old cook arrived with the pothooks that she handed to Big Tom. There was a hook for hanging bacon high up on the chimneybreast. Big Tom stuck the two hooks of the pothooks into Devious Devil's neck each side of his jaw bones, hung him on the high hook, tied his hands behind his back, stuffed a rag in his mouth and threw water in his face to wake him. Then he gently picked up his dead Mary and carried her away and buried her in the same grave as his mother.

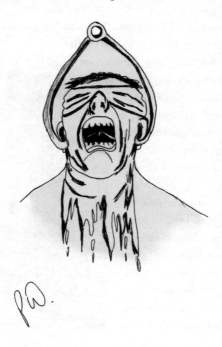

Meanwhile, the old cook dampened the dirty cloth in Devious Devil's mouth, so that he would not die too soon. She gathered up all his ill-gotten money, stuffed it in her apron and then closed the door of the den. Then she sent word to the still living victims of Devious Devil, who all came by night and, literally, had a piece of him and his confiscated money. The money they kept, the pieces they fed to their dogs. He lasted two days and when he died, the old cook cut him up, cooked the pieces in a big pot held by the pothooks and fed them to the pigs.

The next day, Big Tom came to thank the cook for her help and to say goodbye, as he could see no reason to remain in this world. The old cook took his arm, 'If that's the way you are going don't go empty-handed. The master will be home this evening and you could bring him for company on your journey. He always comes down here alone to inspect everything first thing.' She handed Big Tom a lump hammer that he took with a determined grimace. The master never knew what hit him. The soldiers shot Big Tom Ward twenty times. He was buried with the two loves of his life. There they rest in peace. The old cook was found dead on the bog road the next day. She was buried with her son, daughter and unborn grandchild. They too rest there in peace.

The not so Devious Devil's ghost, complete with pothooks that look like a black devil's halo, it still roams some nights around the ruins of the Roscommon Castles. Some say that he is still suffering. Others say that you have to be very good or very bad to see him. Have you seen him? If so which sort are you? What about the master, is his ghost wandering on its way to hell? No, he went directly – he was hot before he was cold.

☙❧

James O'Kelly was from a later time. He was known as James J., and, unlike his ancestors who inherited or seized power, he was elected by the people to represent them in the palaces of power. He was trained as a blacksmith, worked in Dublin and London and when he met John Devoy he became involved in The Irish Brotherhood in 1860. He left to study in Paris, joined the French Foreign Legion and saw action in Algiers and Mexico. There, he was wounded and taken prisoner. He escaped and arrived back in London in 1863 where he heard that the Fenians were planning armed insurrection. As he was an experienced solder, he knew that the poorly trained and very poorly armed Irish had no chance. He did not take part. He later used the martyrdom of those killed to inspire others.

After the rising failed and the Fenians were killed, jailed or scattered he became a Supreme Council member of the IRB (Irish Republican Brotherhood). He built up this organisation in Ireland and England. When France got involved in the Prussian war he went to rejoin their army as a captain but he resigned when Paris fell. He then became a journalist with the *Irishman*, a Dublin paper. In 1871 he got a job in London with the *New York Herald*. All this time he was in correspondence with John Devoy, the Fenian leader who had escaped to America. He went to Cuba as a war correspondent, got behind Spanish lines, got captured and was sentenced to death. However, the British got him a pardon and he returned and wrote a book about his exploits. By this time he had convinced Devoy to support Charles Stuart Parnell, a conservative Nationalist member of parliament.

In 1879, he returned to Roscommon and was selected with three others to contest the 1890 election. His vast experience of the world and of journalism saw him elected ahead of the O'Conor Don, a descendent of the Connaught kings, despite the intervention of Dr Gillooly, Bishop of Elphin. This was a Land League victory as the peasants were convinced that it was possible to get ownership of their land. There was a bonfire for him on the bridge in Castlerea. In October of that year, there were 40,000 at a Land League meeting in Boyle where O'Kelly spoke with experience, eloquence and the authority of an army leader. He exhorted all to join the League to great enthusiastic applause. Similar meetings in Roscommon and Athlone followed this. O'Kelly's call was 'Get rid of the foreign landlords and down with landlordism.'

Following this, there was a Coercion Act of Parliament passed with evictions, jailing, and considerable aggravation between peasants and the powers that be. It was more than twenty years before the Land League bore fruit. After Parnell's troubled death, O'Kelly stayed with the party under Redmond until his death in 1916. He was revered in Boyle where he donated a pulpit to the church and they even have a football club named for him: 'The Kilronan O'Kellys'.

18

THE LEGEND

Peter called a family conference. He, his wife Mary and their seven children lived on a thirty-acre rented farm in Co Armagh, near Lough Neagh. They had moved there from Scotland when they got married twenty-five-years ago. The landlord there was a cousin of the laird, who their father rented landed from beside Lough Lomond. They had got the farm there on account of their expert knowledge of flax growing and processing. The children consisted of young Peter, Mary, James, John, Patrick, Ester and Maud.

Peter spoke and all listened: 'In my grandfather's time our family were comfortable farmers near Lincoln in England. That was when the Protestant Reformation arrived and, as we wanted to remain true to the Catholic faith, we had to abandon our farm there and, luckily, a Scottish laird took us in as tenants. We managed fine there without too much trouble for two generations but, by then the Reformation had caught up with us again so the laird sent us here. We had a fair bit of hassle here in the early years for being from abroad but, after Patrick was christened with neighbouring godparents, we were accepted as Irish Catholics. Now, Rome has sent King James to raise an army in Ireland to defeat King William and restore the Catholic monarchy in Ireland and England. King James is arriving in Dublin in the next few days and he wants all the young Catholic men in Ireland to rally to his cause. It is decision time for this family. Do we keep running before the Protestant Reformation or do we whole-heartedly support King James, Rome and God?'

'What does that mean?' asked John.

'It means,' replied his father, 'that three of you should go south to Dublin and join James's army.' All four boys immediately volunteered. Their mother was devastated and fearful but proud of her sons.

'Peter will have to stay to help with the farm,' said the father, 'but I would be glad if James, John and Patrick went.' After some protest from Peter, this was agreed. Then they all knelt and prayed.

The next day the three boys joined up with a great many others who were also heading for Dublin. As they went, there was considerable jeering from Protestants that they encountered. When they reached Dublin and joined James's army, they were dismayed at the poverty-stricken appearance of the Gaelic-speaking Irish from the rest of the country. They were poorly armed and had only two big guns. However, they had great numbers and the promise of more when they progressed. The year was 1690. There were several fancily-dressed kings, generals and leaders who looked like peacocks, and it was difficult for the brothers or the peasants to distinguish one from the other. They wondered if they could possibly be fighting for Ireland.

Major Owen O'Conor addressed the gathering. As the crowd was so big, he spoke in short sentences and paused after each sentence so that his words could be relayed to those out of earshot. He was extremely well kitted out and he said that he was O'Conor Don, a direct descendant of the last High King of Ireland, Rory. He said he was there to lead, with the assistance of all those assembled, to restore the Catholic Church in Ireland and, afterwards, in England. He said that, with God's help, he would undo the terrible damage that the Reformation has done throughout Ireland and England and the Continent. He also promised that when he became High King of Roscommon, Connaught and Ireland, all the churches and monasteries would be restored and reopened for proper Catholic Mass and devotion.

'We are fighting for God and country,' he said, to a great cheer and waving of weapons.

Then all headed north.

King William and his army, along with twenty-six big guns, met them at the Boyne River. James's plan was to stop them crossing the river and, to this end, he spread his army a few miles along the south side. The Williamites made a serious effort to cross at just one point, exactly where the three brothers were defending. Guns were fired first, then it was hand-to-hand fighting in the water, with blood, sweat, fear, courage, luck, guts and death until the river ran red with the blood of 1,500 men. Miraculously, though fiercely blooded and bloodied, the three brothers escaped with only flesh wounds, that were not fatal.

The whole Irish army retreated to Athlone, where they hoped to stop the Williamites at the bigger River Shannon. There was also a castle on the west side. After crossing the river, the Irish destroyed two spans of the bridge and dug in on the Connaught side. In spite of the big guns, better arms, better trained soldiers and better leadership, the Jacobites failed to take the bridge for a full year. Neither side were prepared for this long stand-off. Food became very scarce. The three brothers, as well as others, were sent out through Roscommon to acquire food and reinforcements for the battle. The Catholic landlords were most helpful. One Loughlin Naughten gave vast amounts of food and recruited 100 men from among his tenants to help in the battle. The experienced, battle-hardened men trained those recruits and armed them as best they could. One night, the Williamites succeeded in throwing heavy planks across the broken-down spans of the bridge and at dawn as they attempted to cross twenty brave Irish men rushed into the gunfire and threw the planks into the river. They were blown to pieces, with blood, bone and guts spattering the planks as they fell. Only two survived, swimming to safety. The battle was nearly won, as those on the Leinster side had devoured everything in sight and were now nearly starving. But luck was on their side. It was a very fine summer and the Shannon was running low, the Jacobites got to walk across the river arm-in-arm at night, as it was only waist-deep. Major O'Conor and his immediate supporters were the only defenders near the bridge but they were taken unaware by the army who walked across the Shannon. They were quickly over-powered, and what was worse, Major Owen was captured. When word of his capture reached the other leaders, they feared greatly for his safety, as they knew he would not on any account give up his religion, even if his life depended on it. It did. He did not. He was dead in a week.

The Irish fell back to Aughrim, where their defensive efforts again failed and many more were killed. They then went on to Limerick, where they finally surrendered.

After the surrender, Naughten, who was captain of the remain-der of his hundred men, was offered a pardon for himself and his men if he turned Protestant and swore allegiance to the English King and Parliament. This he did, as the alternative was death for all. He was also allowed to keep his extensive lands in Roscommon and Galway. As the three brothers, John, who had a broken leg, James and Patrick were now traumatised, broke, injured, homeless and, being Catholic, stranded forever in the wilds of Irish-speaking Roscommon, Naughten took them in as tenants on little farms. Quite a number of the defeated army were treated the same way and Roscommon got a new type of English, different to any who came before, as these had to start off as poor tenants, mostly on land much inferior to what they were used to. They also had to adapt to a new and difficult environment, customs and land, and many also had to learn the language or at least, adjust to the local dialect, but because they were Catholics, they were usually welcomed. Of course, the failed soldiers could not risk commu-nicating with their families who remained at home as they would have been punished if the authorities became aware of the family involvement in the uprising. Like many before them, they soon became more Irish than the Irish themselves. Those were the last

group of English people to come to Roscommon and they were grateful for what they got and took nothing by force. Many of them brought new farming methods and, in some cases, new crops to Roscommon.

The last few of O'Conor's men had joined Naughten and, after they were pardoned, they hobbled back to north-west Roscommon, where they too started subsistence farming.

Luckily, relations of Major Owen O'Conor, with the same bloodline, inherited the title and held limited lands and faith, through penal times, famine and frugality so that today they reside in Clonalis House and have it open to the public every summer.

19

THE STORY
OF ROSCOMMON'S
HANG WOMAN

After the battles of the Boyne, Athlone and Aughrim in 1690-91, the depleted Catholic forces surrendered at Limerick. Extreme penal laws were passed that took away all rights from the Catholic Irish. Landlords were given absolute power to charge whatever rent they wished and were free to evict tenants at any time, for any or no reason. Catholics were denied any type of education, religious service, assembly, or representation in any forum. Priests were banned and there was a reward on their heads. Some landlords were fairly reasonable while others were absolute despots. Some of the Roscommon landlords had up to 30,000 acres. They owned town and country.

An illustration of what dreadful, depraved and inhuman things happened in one lifetime is the story of Lady Betty of Roscommon, who was originally from Kerry. Betty, who was unusual because she was able to read, married Michael Healy in Kerry in the middle of the eighteenth century. They had a twenty-acre farm rented from a reasonable landlord and they had two farm boys employed. Part of Betty's dowry were two books that she used to teach Michael to read. The payment for the farm boys was in part the use of an acre each to grow their own food. There was great joy when the young couple had a son who they named Padraig, after his grandfather. A second son, Michael Oge, arrived a year later. A third pregnancy coincided with the death of the landlord. His wayward son, who had a gambling problem, inherited the land.

The new landlord immediately doubled the rent, and when the family were not able to pay, they were evicted and, as a result of the trauma, Betty lost the third baby. The landlord was aware that the family had some friends and relations who were prepared to give a little help. Therefore, he offered them a much smaller farm, on poorer land at the same rent. As it was springtime and the beginning of the growing season they took it and paid the rent in advance. As the farm boys were gone, Michael assisted by Betty with her baby and toddler, tilled the little farm with hand tools and sowed a crop of potatoes. As soon as the sowing was finished, the landlord doubled the rent again, with the second half due immediately. When they were not able to pay they were evicted again. This was when the two Michaels got sick and died within hours of each other. The very last of Betty's possessions, save the two books, went to pay for their burials in their native Kerry.

Betty and her toddler son, Padraig, then went begging. For a few years the Kerry people kept them alive. But, as times got harder, the beggars had to go farther afield, to Limerick. At this stage, Betty told Padraig that as they had left Kerry, they would now change their names to Sullivan. Because Padraig was only a lad, he saw nothing wrong with this. As they begged their way across Limerick, Betty became more disillusioned and Padraig, who had then learned to read and write a little, took over the management of their affairs. His mother used to do writing for people but then it was Padraig who took up the business of asking in every house and village if anyone wanted any reading done or letters written. When he got his first job, to read a letter from America, he struggled but Betty took it from him and they read it together. When answering the letter they did the same. Padraig was delighted to get his mother partly out of the malady of silence into which she had sunk and the letter people fed them paid them a little and got them another job with a neighbour. Sometimes they went days without any job but when they did get reading and writing Padraig noticed that it not only helped their bellies, finance, and his education, but it always awoke his mother from her sulk. When they crossed the Shannon into Clare, Betty announced that they must change their name to O'Connell. Padraig accepted. Things went the same there and they begged and worked all the way to Gort in County Galway. This time they changed their name to O'Shea and when they went through Ballinasloe into Roscommon, their name became Sugrue. By this time, Padraig, although very young, had perfected the art of getting reading jobs but Betty had lost the will to live. He, at a tender age, had to procure all their needs. As he watched his mother sink deeper into depression and despair, every day he told her that he would look after her and that, one day, he would see to it that she would have all she needs. In Roscommon, Padraig got many little jobs because he was able to read and they were able to rent a tiny hovel to live in. When he was eighteen, with his meagre savings, he bought her a book that they both read every day. The other two books had been sold long ago for food.

One day, the soldiers called looking for Padraig and he had to sail for America to escape them. Betty's world was turned upside-down. Padraig arrived just in time for the War of Independence and was seized and conscripted into the English army. He soon deserted and joined Washington's forces with his gun and ammunition. After the war, he sent a letter with money and said that he was going out west. He never wrote again and Betty, who loved him dearly, thought that he was dead and went into a permanent depression and deep anger with God. By doing odd jobs, some very odd, and eating very frugally, not by choice, she was able to keep her humble abode.

Many years later, on a very wet cold winter night, a loud knock on her door woke her. When she opened the door, there was a very wet, grey-haired, middle-aged man there with his horse. 'May I and my horse stay here tonight?' he asked. She decided that there was a chance to eke out a few pennies so she agreed but pointed out that she had nothing to eat in the house. From a pouch he pulled a sovereign and bid her get food. She was impressed and hurried away. When she had procured the food and fed him in silence, he asked to sleep in her bed and let her stay by the fire. Thinking of the sovereigns, she agreed and soon he was fast asleep. Then she sought out and searched his pouch. She found a hoard of sovereigns that would keep her in luxury for the rest of her life. After some thought, she considered stabbing the stranger to death and stealing the gold. She wrestled with her conscience for some time but, finally, she told God that He treated her bad all her life. He took everything she had. He took everyone she loved. He took her husband. He took her sons. He took her home twice. He made her life a misery. He turned her and her son into beggars. He could do no more to her. But now, He expected her to keep His laws.

'I just won't,' she said. She killed the stranger.

Later, she found that God could do much worse to her and that she had murdered her long lost son Padraig.

Words were not adequate to describe her grief, anger, sorrow, despair, guilt and self-loathing. She went roaring up the town. People thought she was mad. They were right. She was arrested, tried, found guilty and sentenced to be hanged in Roscommon jail. At first, she was glad to hear the sentence as it would take her out of her misery, a misery she could not bear. She would be glad to be dead, to get away from this accursed county, country, cruelty and life. Then she went into a rage at herself, God, all the saints, and everybody in the world. She decided to resist everything the authorities would try to do. She would go to the gallows screaming and kicking to the last. When her hands and feet were

tied, she would spit at them, shout at them and create as much stink as possible and try everything to make them kill her before she reached the gallows. She would give them and the entire gawking crowd something to remember. She did.

The day for hanging her and several others arrived but the hangman died suddenly that morning. There was consternation among the authorities. There was no hangman available, nor could one be found. Betty declared that, if she was granted a pardon, she would hang the others. After some debate, her offer was accepted and she became Lady Betty, Roscommon's hang woman.

Ironically, her tragic son Padraig had finally kept his promise and brought her enough wealth to have shelter over her head and enough to eat every day for the remainder of her life.

20

LANDLORDS

During the eighteenth century, landlords built over seven thousand big houses, in many cases mini castles, financed by rents from tenants, many of whom were nearly starving. Needless to say, many of those were in Roscommon, where some of the biggest estates in the country could be found. During this time wool became scarce and sheep were capable of producing more money per acre for the landlords than peasants. Tenants were evicted from large tracts of the best land that was then being laid out in big fields, suitable for sheep farming. Sometimes the tenants were offered poorer wetter land or cut away bog where sheep would not survive. They took those lands, as they had no alternative. From bitter experience a saying arose among the peasantry:

> There is gold to be found under gorse,
> silver under rushes
> and hunger under heather.

Potatoes will grow on good land where gorse grows, less well on rushy land but not at all where there is heather. Sheep are the same.

Denis Mahon was one of many influential landlords and he had ten thousand acres near Strokestown. Like others in famine times, he had many small poor tenants who were unable to pay their rents. At this time, the government brought out a grant of money to help landlords to remove tenants in very congested areas. This was done by persuading poor tenants to accept passage to Canada. Mahon and his agent, another Mahon (no relation), persuaded 1,000 people, including tenants and families, to go. Between leaving Strokestown and arriving in Canada, half of them died and the rest were very ill. Over the following months in quarantine there, another 200 died. Only 300 lived to try and make a new life in Canada. When word of this reached Strokestown, everybody was appalled. The fact that those 1,000 people were the poorest of the poor and that, if they had not gone, many of them would have died anyway, was not taken into account. The fact that two thousand six hundred others were also evicted, with nowhere to go added to the grievances of their friends, relations and neighbours. There was outrage against the landlord and dark mutterings among many. In spite of this, the poor were not able to retaliate, as they were sad, sore, sorry, scared and, in most cases, underfed. One of Denis Mahon's enemies, who was from the gentry, and who stood to gain from his death, shot Denis Mahon dead. This caused outrage among the landed and governing classes and there was considerable harassment and abuse of the peasants. Two of them were soon arrested, charged, found guilty and hanged.

The dead Denis lay in state on a linen sheet that was spread on a table in the extensive front hall of his mansion. The tenants had to walk humbly through the front door in single-file round the coffin and out again, praying for him as they went and showing as much grief as possible. Yes, they all prayed but not all prayed for his salvation!

Over a hundred and thirty years later the last of the Mahons were living in very poor circumstances in just one room of their decaying mansion, the only room not leaking. A local man bought the lot and the last Mahon died shortly after in Dublin.

The new owner restored the house and gardens and opened it to the public so they could see the grandeur in which the gentry once lived. More importantly, today he has a famine museum in

memory of all that died and suffered at that time. Even the gun
used to shoot Denis Mahon is on display and, hopefully, it will give
some fierce, fiendish comfort and satisfaction to some and gener-
ate forgiveness and blessings in others. This house is now being
visited by people, mostly of the Roscommon and Irish Diaspora
from all over the world. Indeed, it may be an emotional visit for
many who are descendants of once evicted tenants of this or other
places. May the road rise with them!

ABSENTEE LANDLORDS

Others landlords lived abroad and had agents in Ireland to collect
rents and run their estates. Some of those had estates in England
or other parts of Ireland and many of them spent the winter on
the French Rivera. At that time, the potato had become the main
food of peasants and there was a population explosion. Peasants
had large families and divided their smallholdings among their
children. This led to tiny farms and in many areas there were farms
of less than one acre, while others had no land at all and depended
on getting work on larger farms and perhaps getting some food
and a little land on which to grow potatoes. As there was no education, young people had little moral guidance. The Irish spirit was
still in them and they enjoyed, often recklessly, every little pleasure
that came their way. Wakes and weddings were occasions for much
merriment, games, music, trickery and drunkenness. They mar-

ried young and had plenty of children with no planning, but love and hope. Both let them down. There was a saying, 'When hunger comes in the door, love goes out the window'.

As there was no education, a few brave souls, who had been educated, started illegal 'Hedge Schools'. As the name suggests, those 'schools' were under hedges for shelter, in remote places. Volunteers put a few wattles together with a thatched roof to give the scholars and teachers a little shelter. Many got a reasonable education in this manner and, indeed, Irish people who were banished to the new Australian lands with prisoners from other parts of the Empire were the only educated convicts. The same was true of many who went to America.

As ever, the people reverted to writing seditious ballads. This was to keep Irish history, traditions, religion and customs alive. Many ballads were written in praise of dead heroes and highly critical of landlords, their agents, Protestants, England, the Crown and all things English. Other ballads told of murdered priests, burnt churches, demon soldiers, devil landlords, the rotten Crown evictions and the saintly Irish who never did wrong. When they were sung at fairs by a poor evicted, half-starved, poorly clad farmer, standing barefoot in fresh cow dung to keep his bare feet warm, they crept into their minds and enthused the next generation.

However, there was a law passed that made it a hanging offence to write any article in any language or poem containing the words 'Irish', 'Ireland', 'Éire' or 'Éireann'. The bards got round this by using phrases like 'My Dark Rosaleen' or 'My Little Brown Cow', instead. Those ballads were also being sung at weddings and wakes and, as always, the acclaim increased with drink and often led to fisticuffs. As ever, the little people were there, cheering them on.

This is one such poem, 'My Little Brown Cow', was written in Irish during those times and translated to English by an inspired hot-blooded, schoolboy a long time later in 1950:

My sweet Little Brown Cow, cream of the throng
Where spend you your nights and all the days long?
I dwell in the mountains with my young son along
For they over there left me tearful from wrong.
I don't have a home, or food, music or glow,
Nor friends nor comrades nor nowhere to go,
But all day drinking water with spirits so low
While my enemies have wine and whiskey to blow.
But if I got a light or a sight the Crown
England I'd lambast and drag her right down
Through mountains, valleys and glens foggy brown,
That's how I'd treat her, my sweet cow so young.

In 2011, after Queen Elizabeth II visited Ireland on the invitation of the then Irish President, Mary McAleese, who is also of Roscommon origin, the inspired boy, by then an old man, added a last verse:

But when the Queen came with a smile so disarming
And speaking in Irish with phrases so charming
If anything happened it would be so alarming
This lovely old lady we'd never be harming.
Peace has arrived at last.

Catholic emancipation in 1829 started a slow improvement for the Roscommon tenants but the disastrous potato famine of the 1840s was Ireland's greatest misery, with the population of the country and Roscommon falling by half in many places and by a third overall through hunger, disease, eviction and emigration. Many landlords went broke from having over borrowed and being unable to collect rents in poorer times. Ironically, the areas where the tenants were evicted by landlords so they could feed sheep, suffered less in the famine as the population was less dense and the farms were not as small.

The famine changed everything in Ireland. Even many of those who survived had lost faith in the country and emigrated at the first opportunity. Never again were farms divided between siblings; instead all but one emigrated. Many sent home the fare for siblings or dowry money for any who wanted to stay. The emigration to Britain, its colonies and America continued until the end of the twentieth century.

Farmers realised that, for survival, one must own his land or at least have fair rent and not be subject to eviction.

The spirit of Ireland seemed to be dead and forgotten but it returned at the first opportunity. When the Land League was started and Michael Davitt was encouraging people to unite against landlords, a leprechaun whispered these words to the young men of Ireland:

The landlord has made a demand,
To evict all the poor from their land.
But speak Michael Davitt,
We just will not have it
Now the landlord himself we'll get canned.

This encouraged most to join the Land League and there was some coercion where necessary. There was a secret murderous society called White Boys or Ribbon Boys. They held secret trials, in the absence of the accused, of landlords or others accused of unfair treatment of tenants; if found guilty that landlord would have his house burnt or some of his property destroyed, or in extreme cases he might be shot. The perpetrator would then be sent to America to avoid arrest. The chance of a new life in America tempted many a young man to evil deeds.

Inch by painful inch, land reform came, so that by 1920, the Irish Land Commission was in possession of most of the land in Roscommon and Ireland. The land was given permanently to the sitting tenants on a fifty-year buy-out arrangement. Most of the original landlords faded away and disappeared from Roscommon. The few that remained farming ordinary sized farms followed in the footsteps of those before them and became seriously Irish.

A side-effect of the Penal Laws being imposed by the English in Ireland was the loss of America in the War of Independence there. The Irish deserted the English army and fought with Washington's freedom fighters. They also inspired others to do the same through stories, songs, music and hatred of the redcoats. It was said that England lost a continent over the misty Emerald Isle.

General Cornwallace, who was blamed for losing the war in America, was banished to Ireland for his failure. In a strange way, he did do some good in Roscommon and Ireland. He used his soldiers to survey and map every field in Ireland. In order to do this, he trained his soldiers to walk in rows ten feet apart from north to south, stopping every five paces to mark in everything they saw. They marked in every field, fence, house, hill, hollow, river and stream in the country. In this way, Ireland was the first country in the world to have a proper Ordnance Survey map. He also wrote down an anglicised version of every place name.

As there was great fear and mistrust of English soldiers and all things English, there was resistance to them walking through people's fields, yards, homes and every private place. Cornwallace issued an edict that the first day resistance was encountered in an area, the soldiers were to shoot all the dogs. On the second day they were to shoot all the livestock and on the third day of resistance they were to shoot all the men. As everyone knew that he had total power, resistance was never for more than one day and only dogs died. While Cornwallace's work was resisted and severely criticised, especially his changing of place names, it was the only good thing he is remembered for.

21

THE PRICE OF A PRIEST

A whistling woman or a crowing hen calls the Devil out of his den, and everybody knew that hearing either a whistling woman or a crowing hen indicated serious trouble for the family concerned. But if both happened at the same time, that could only mean catastrophe for the family or indeed, for the whole village.

Mary Dolan seemed to be a normal little girl growing up but just when she turned sixteen she started whistling well-known tunes. As they were getting ready for pre-dawn Mass at the rock, Peg, her mother, heard her one morning; she was crestfallen. She blessed herself with holy water, she sprinkled and blessed the girl and then attacked a surprised Mary verbally, in a vicious way that Mary never thought her mother was capable of.

'What harm is it?' she asked in all innocence.

'What harm is it?' said her fuming mother as she sprinkled more holy water. 'Your father must be turning in his grave. It's the devil, that's what it is and it will bring bad luck on you and all the family, so don't ever dare do it again.' Mary said she meant no harm; it was only a bit of sport but if it bothers that much she would not do it again. The mother was doubtful; she had seen this malady and its consequences before but she never thought it would come to her own child. Then she heard it, a strange weird off-key sort of crowing sound. It was not an ordinary 'cock-a-doodle-doodle-do' but more of a 'cock-a-draca-doodle-dy'. Her heart jumped, she turned snow-white,

she broke into a cold sweat, it couldn't be but it was, a crowing hen. This and the whistler!

'We're doomed,' she cried. Peg looked out to see where the accursed hen was. She was standing on one of the two cut-stone peers that her son Matt had recently erected. She told him he should never have taken the stones from that bloody Norman Castle. There was never anything there only mayhem, murder, disease, devastation, destruction, and fierce, fighting factions forever forcing ordinary poor people to die for causes they often scarcely understood. No wonder the place was left desolate for the wild creatures to inhabit. There could be no luck in the stones from there anyway, but to steal them at night, what was Matt thinking? Now look at the trouble they were in.

'Oh God help us!' she said, wringing her hands. She knew when Matt told her that a weasel had spat at him from the castle wall. She knew when the weasel followed Matt home and killed six hens that night. She knew when Matt broke the weasel's head with a blackthorn stick that no good would come from it. Of course, the Devil from hell made sure that the weasel did not kill the hen that was going to crow. Maybe the weasel was the Devil. Now the Devil had his way. 'Oh God, his Blessed Mother and St Joseph help us,' she wailed.

When Matt came home he met a very angry mother, who castigated him for getting notions of himself. Nothing would do him but two cut-stone peers and an iron gate like the gentry.

'We were better off when we had the heap of manure outside the front door hiding the house and giving bailiffs and landlords the impression that we lived in shit, had nothing and knew nothing. Just because you broke a few horses for Crofton, Coote and Mahon does not make you a gentleman. Just because you gelded a few horses and none died does not make you a gentleman. Just because you won a few steeplechases does not make you a gentleman. Just because you have an understanding with the gentry that you are Roscommon's most knowledgeable horseman does not make you a gentleman.'

'Whoa, whoa woman, what are you talking about?' asked Matt as soon as he could get a word in edgeways. Just then, the hen flew on to a peer and started to crow.

'Now you know,' said Peg. 'That hen will be the death of you and that's not the half of it, Mary is whistling,' she said, bursting into tears. He took her shaking, sobbing body in his arms and just held her tight.

'There, there,' he said, for he could think of nothing else to say. The double whammy shook Matt, leaving him speechless. He was not easily shaken, for, so far, he had made a great success of his life and that was not easy when dealing with the land-grabbing tyrannical English and their Redcoats doing their dirty work. He had

lived by his wits always, but he could think of no solution to this
unearthly problem. If it was only the hen he could pull her neck
and dump her on someone else's land to get rid of the bad luck.
Better still he could take her to Mahon's land and pull her neck and
bury her there so that no bit of bad luck would stay with him or his
family. But his darling little sister Mary whistling at the same time,
that made a whole new situation and he did not know what to do.
However, he did know that any injury he inflicted on the hen, that
same thing might happen to Mary. He was the oldest and, since
his father died many years ago, he was the man of the house. He
would ask his cousin, the priest, for advice and divine intervention
if possible.

'Here, take this,' said Matt as he handed his mother his money
pouch, containing a great number of sovereigns. 'Both of you go to
the Mass Rock by the fields and don't ever come back here. There's
enough money there to get you both to America and set you up
well there. I will stay here and do what has to be done.' The mother
nodded, hugged him tight, whispering in his ear, 'God bless you
Matt.' She took the bag in one hand and Mary by the other hand
and both disappeared into the night.

Thirty years before, although the handy woman had to be rushed
the hundred yards from one house to the other to birth the first
cousins within the hour, they were a decade apart. Peter Pious
Dolan came quietly into the world at three minutes to twelve on
the night of 31 December 1749, while his cousin Matt arrived kicking and screaming one hour later on 1 January 1750. Peter Pious
had to be severely slapped on the bottom to get him to cry enough
to clear his lungs; he seldom cried again and was always quiet and
studious. Matt, on the other hand, was wild and flamboyant from
the very start. Their fathers, who were twin brothers, were unalike
in every way and this was repeated in their sons who were born in
different decades.

As they grew and attended the same hedge school, the 'loving
enmity' that was always evident between their fathers was again

manifest in the cousins. This difference was made worse by Matt who always referred to Peter Pious as 'old man from the last decade, too old to laugh or play'. Peter Pious's gentle retort was always the same: 'There's no manners on you, Matt Dolan.'

At school, to which they walked barefoot three miles daily together, they were both bright children. The schoolmaster was glad to have such talent and while he always had Peter Pious tagged as a priest; Matt was full of devilment and had to be verbally and often physically disciplined. During his time at school every insect, creepy crawly, flying creature or furry little animal from the parish also attended at one time or another, much to the annoyance of the girls, the amusement of the boy's and the anger of the master, and Matt was always responsible. But for all that, he was the life and soul of the school.

On the way home in the evenings, Peter Pious walked at a steady pace, with little interest in his surroundings. They did not carry books except a work copy concealed inside their clothing, as their schooling was illegal activity. Unlike his cousin, Matt was fascinated by everything he saw and he either examined it, jumped on it, threw stones at it or, if it was edible, bit it or stole it altogether. In harvest, no apple, plum, gooseberry or pear was safe and even a cake left outside on a window to cool could be minus a bite. In winter, raw turnips and even potatoes could suffer. Nobody begrudged them, as priests were scarce and there was promise in the cousins.

At that time, people had very little land and it was not unusual for some to graze the side of the road with some quiet animal that would not stray. Tim had such a pony and he lived half a mile from the two scholars. One morning, Matt jumped on the grazing pony and rode it bareback to within a hundred yards of the school, where he dismounted and abandoned the steed. Peter Pious was horrified as he ran behind foretelling all sorts of imminent trouble. Nothing untoward happened. The pony headed for home but as there was better grazing here, he took his time. In the evening, the boys caught up with him a mile from the school. Matt mounted the animal again and persuaded Peter Pious to ride behind him, holding on to Matt for dear life. After several days, Tim found out what was happening but he was not bothered, only asking that the pony would be left to him on market day. So thereafter, they rode to school, four out of five days. Matt was a natural horseman and jockey but, over a few years, even Peter Pious became a proficient jockey. This would prove very useful in later life.

When they finished school, Peter Pious was smuggled out to the continent where, fourteen years later he was ordained a priest. Meanwhile, Matt had made a name for himself as a gifted horseman, who could break any young horse perfectly so he would never stop, stag or throw his rider. When he started winning point-to-point races, the gentry took notice and Mahon, Coote and Crofton were quick to give him commissions to buy promising young horses for them. To this end, he travelled to fairs over several counties and got a bit richer than his neighbours, so much so that he thought it appropriate to clean up the front of his house and build stone peers with an iron gate. He had arrived.

Two years before this, Peter Pious had returned as a priest-on-the-run. On a very wet January day, Matt was at a fair in Roscommon and, as always, he was busy with everyone wanting to talk to him. If it was not gentry on horseback, it was some poor farmer looking to have a horse examined for wind, bots, stop, stag, curb, halt or mange. He worked free for the peasants but the gentry would pay through an increased price for their next horse. When a scraggy-looking poor bearded man with a stick quietly asked Matt to get him a horse and Matt looked him in the eye, he recognised Peter Pious. He kept his cool.

'Be walking outside the town in an hour and don't speak to me unless I have a spare horse.' Peter Pious shuffled off and no one noticed.

'Jump up there,' said Matt, an hour later, as he handed Peter Pious the reins of his spare horse. 'You're a horse dealer from Sligo coming to my house for the night, if anyone asks.' As stonewalls had ears, they rode in silence.

Very soon Matt had arranged lodgings in safe houses and given the horse to the priest. That horse would be kept on different farms and would always be neglected-looking and dirty in order to look like a farm horse.

Some time before that, Crofton's daughter was getting married and, of course, she would arrive at the church in a coach-and-six. Now, Crofton had a pair of black horses, each with four white legs, like socks that he used for his buggy. He commissioned Matt to scour the country for four similar horses to make six for the marriage carriage. Matt travelled widely from Meath to Dublin to Cork and back through Clare and Galway. He got the four white-socked horses much to the delight of Crofton and the profit of Matt.

He also got another young horse for himself. This one he thought would be a winner. He was black colt with a white star on his forehead. Matt trained him, groomed him, named him Flyby and won every race on him. He was famous and unbeatable.

At that time, there was a £5 reward for a dead priest but the gentry and the soldiers, mostly, did not enforce this. However, the law was there and a certain Captain Mathews was determined to do his duty and rid the county of meddling priests. Many were convinced that he was a descendant of Cromwell; otherwise he could not be so vicious. He got wind of the arrival of Peter Pious and thereafter he led four-soldier-patrols throughout the area night and day.

Matt decided that Peter Pious was in danger and needed a faster horse so that, if it ever came to a chase, the priest could outrun the Redcoats. The next steeplechase he competed in, he fell at the first jump and lost the race. Not only that but he announced that his shoulder was injured and that he would not race again for a long time. The real reason for this was that he had found a horse that looked like Flyby, but of course he was just ordinary and would never be a winner. Matt groomed him exactly the same as Flyby and pretended it was the same horse. Meanwhile, he cut Flyby's tail, hid him in a wood to get scruffy-looking and painted his white star black. A few weeks later, Peter Pious was riding the camouflaged Flyby.

Matt's fears were well founded. One dawn, just as the priest was mounting his horse after Mass on the rock, Captain Mathews and his three minions came galloping. While the ragged congregation scattered among the rocks, Peter Pious mounted Flyby and they went like the wind. The Redcoats confidently followed but, after a mile, the priest was nearly out of sight so they gave up.

'Blimey, the ruddy priest's 'ose is magic then,' said Ray, the private from London. Mathews hit him a vicious back hander with his whip across the face, knocking him from his horse.

'You stupid bloody fool, you're talking the same stupid superstition as the filthy peasants. Get on your horse and don't ever let me hear you or any of His Majesty's soldiers speak such nonsense again.' As they rode home a very angry captain vowed to himself that the rogue who misled the fools would not best him again.

After his mother and sister left to go to the Mass rock, Matt got the bucket and went to the well for water. By the time he arrived back he felt faint and, leaving down the bucket of water, he sat on the windowsill to catch his breath. Matt and his mother knew that he had to drown the crowing hen at dawn. What his mother did not know was that Matt had been feeling bad for a few days, that yesterday he had been coughing up blood and that last night he got a bad fit of coughing and a lot of blood came. For the first time in his life he felt weary, and he was hot and sweaty as he sat there in the predawn.

Peter Pious decided that in future all Masses would be celebrated two-hours before dawn so that he and his people could get home under the cover of darkness. He should have anticipated that the captain would expect just such a move. On the very night that the trouble had arrived at Matt's door, just as Peter Pious was finishing his next Mass, they first heard and then saw the outlines of horses coming fast. The priest jumped on Flyby and galloped away. The people scattered. The soldiers followed Flyby. Just as Peter Pious was passing Matt's house, the crowing hen fluttered onto the peer to crow. The horse swerved throwing the priest over the wall on the far side of the lane. He banged his head and blacked out. The horse stopped with his reins dragging on the ground, just as Matt arrived out from where he sat and picked up the reins. The soldiers arrived round the corner. 'Shoot!' shouted the angry captain. Matt and Flyby fell dead.

When the priest awoke he heard talking from the far side of the wall.

'It's bloody Matt the horseman,' the captain was saying, as he lifted Matt's head by the hair. When he dropped the head with a thud the priest knew that his cousin, friend, tormenter and wonderful benefactor was dead. Through tears he held his breath.

'That's why we couldn't catch the bugger. Look, it's Flyby with his star painted. Matt, the bastard, was the priest all the time. Who would have thought? Well, the meddling, conniving bastard is dead now. Fire the house, as I want to erase everything that the two-timing Matt stood for. Now the beggars will know who's the boss and who runs this God-forsaken country.' While the three soldiers were setting fire to the house the covetous captain searched Matt's clothes for the gold that he felt Matt should have. Disgusted, he kicked the corpse. When the thatch was ablaze he said, 'Nothing more for us here, mount up.'

After they were gone the sad and grateful priest gave the last rites to his Matt.

'Thanks for everything,' he whispered, 'especially my life.' Then he crept away.

Among the people of the parish and the whole county there was consternation and unrest.

A few days later, when word of the night's happening reached the powers that be, the gentry were concerned and disappointed but a little sad for the loss of Matt who they genuinely liked, not just for him, but for their own stable of horses. They were also baffled as to how Matt could have led a double life so successfully, laughing, joking, riding, training and dealing by day and doing his illegal priestly thing by night. It was a pity, they thought, that a man so talented was not one of theirs. They were also concerned by rumours of reprisals. There were none, as Fr Peter Pious told the people that, in his opinion, Matt had died a martyr and was now a saint. Matt's mother and sister made it to America where they joined those who had gone before and Matt's gold gave them all a head start.

When the fire started, all the hens fled cackling and fluttering across the fields where they were soon devoured by the grateful foxes. Perhaps the full foxes were crowing to their friends about it!

Captain Mathews and the four soldiers were sent back to England. Thereafter, while priests were still officially banned, in practice they were tolerated and Fr Peter Pious ministered to the people for fifty years, the last few after Catholic emancipation in 1829.

He never did hear about the whistling girl or the weird hen.

And what did the peasants say of Captain Mathews? 'May his cat eat him and then, may the Devil eat the cat and then, he will be in little chewed itchy bits inside the cat, inside the Devil, inside hell.'

22

ROSCOMMON AND IRELAND'S
FIRST PRESIDENT

His name was Douglas Hyde and he was from Frenchpark. He was a Protestant and did not attend school as his father, who was a rector, taught him at home. He was always better dressed than his neighbours, as most other families in the area were poor. At that time, Protestants were not Irish speakers, but Douglas was intrigued by the gamekeeper, Seamus Hart, who influenced him greatly and imbued him with the spirit of the Tuatha Dé Danann. This happened as they spent long days together walking through the woods and especially the day Douglas crawled into the Cave of Cats and scratched his name there. Alas, Seamus died suddenly when Douglas was only fourteen, and that spirit seemed to wane but it surfaced again when he was a fellow in Trinity College, Dublin.

Legend has it that he was fascinated with the history and remains of Rindoon castle and that he may have thought thus about it.

The fort at Rindoon was first built by ancient tribes that lived in Roscommon, as they could see that it was easily defended from land or water. It was the forerunner of forts that were built here by every tribe, troop or territory snatcher that visited the Roscommon side of the lake. Ailill and Queen Maeve had a defended landing point here. The Christians later used this landing point for boating to their many island settlements. This facility was brutally taken from them by the hairy, horny, foreign, frightening, fighting Vikings, who just appeared in huge dragon-headed boats on the lake. Over the following years, this landing point changed hands many times between the Vikings and the Kings of Connaught. After the Vikings were gone the Christians and the Connaught Kings shared the facility, most of the time harmoniously, but there were occasional bloody spats between rival Connaught and Uí Maine Kings, the O'Kellys and O'Conors. Various abbots, from time to time, assisted one side or the other. However, it was the Normans who turned Rindoon into a stone city with castles, churches, defences and dwelling places for a great many people. Again, it changed hands between the Normans and the O'Conor Kings many times, and it was considered at least as important as Athlone. But it had not and never could have a bridge across the Shannon. For this reason, the time came when it was totally abandoned with its castles, churches and keeps crumbling, decaying and falling apart. It returned to a remote rural farming area with little memory or mention of its colourful past. It had no part in the eventual freedom of Ireland, nor was it of much interest to Ireland and Roscommon's new rulers. Even now, the ruins are impressive especially the town wall that extends 600 yards across the peninsula. It still stands proud, fourteen-feet high with four impressive gun emplacements. The position of this wall, several hundred yards from the crumbling castle, shows the vast extent of the town that stood between the two. It is incredible that over 2,000 people lived in this town at a time when the population of London was only 15,000. The outline of the slipway used for launching newly built boats is still impressive in its size and layout. The Protestant graveyard is also interesting, having the remains of Oliver Goldsmith's sister, who was the wife of Samuel Jackson. The oldest legible gravestone in Ireland, dating back to the 1300s, is also here.

Rindoon is unusual in having being abandoned while other cities were built over again and again. For this reason, it must be regarded as an ideal location for archaeological investigation, inspection, examination and estimation so that the people who live now and later will better understand what happened in the past. It should be preserved as the unique heritage of Roscommon, its kings, conquerors, defenders, fighting men and peoples. Amazingly, there was never a word of anyone having seen ghosts or anything supernatural here.

After this, Douglas renewed his interest in the Irish language, heritage, ancient history, myths and all things Irish, and was instrumental in forming the 'Conradh na Gaeilge' Gaelic League in 1893. Its purpose was to promote everything Irish including language, music, poetry, ancient history and Gaelic games. He wrote and published scores of Irish poems and he helped to establish the *Gaelic Journal* whose aim was to de-anglicise the Irish nation, arguing that it should follow its own traditions and language. To this end, he published over a hundred articles under the pen name An Craoibhin Aobhinn (The Pleasant Little Branch). He researched and published all the old Gaelic stories, myths and folklore. As well as the Irish language, which was dying at that time, he revived Irish dancing and music that was then only practiced by the poor western people. If it had not been for him, the Irish culture would be much poorer, if not lost altogether. Less than a hundred years later, Irish songs, music and dance are admired and practiced in many places and *Riverdance* is worldwide phenomenon. Many others, who were in this movement, were inspired by him and learned from him, and later went on to revolution, death, martyrdom and finally freedom. The survivors of the revolution later became leaders in the new Irish Free State. Earlier, when some of them suggested using physical force to achieve the ends he espoused, he rejected the method but retained the aims. When he resigned from the presidency of the organisation in 1915, Eoin MacNeill replaced him.

As the others got on with revolution, fighting and dying, he stood aside while retaining the original ideas. When the first Irish Government came to power, they were able to begin to restore the language and culture, only because of the earlier inspired and learned efforts of Douglas. Twenty-three years later, after much fighting, trauma, civil war and political manoeuvring, Eamon De Valera and Liam Cosgrave, opposing party leaders, requested Douglas Hyde to become Ireland's first President and he accepted. There were several reasons why they picked Douglas but the main reason was that all parties and all the people accepted him, and so Roscommon got the nation's first President. This was the nearest thing to a High King that the Irish Free State could get and it was appropriate that, like the last High King, the president was a Roscommon man.

During his seven-year tenure he united the country and carried out the duties of his office with grace and distinction, meeting, greeting and impressing many world leaders. He has many Irish schools called after him and the Roscommon Gaelic Football headquarters at Dr Hyde Park Roscommon and the Hyde Museum in Frenchpark. He was the only Irish leader who had his image on an Irish currency note, £50.

FROM TACHMACONNELL TO ELPHIN

In the southwest of Roscommon we find Tachmaconnell (St Ronans). The place name has outlasted the house and family it was called after. It used to be called Maigh Fin, the land of birches, as there was many birch trees there. Before this parish descends to the river Suck in the west we find the Breole hills that stretch all the way to Dysart.

In the penal times, a very clever boy from Castlesampson, Tachmaconnell, probably travelled across the bog daily to a hedge school in Curraghleen. His name was John Gately Downey and he went to join his sisters in America with his family, when he was just fourteen years old in 1842. Because of a good basis, he was able to continue his education for another two years in America. He worked and gained skills and knowledge in Washington,

Cincinnati, Ohio, Vicksburg, Mississippi, Havana, Cuba, New Orleans, Louisiana, Grass Valley and finally San Francisco. Here, he had a drug store (chemist's shop), and he became so successful that he eventually owned 45,000 acres of land. He also became the first Governor of California to be born outside of America. While governor he vetoed the Bulkhead Bill against the will of many capitalists friends and supporters. In doing so, he showed that not only would the Bill be unconstitutional but also that it would do irreparable damage to the future development of trade and commerce in the developing San Francisco metropolis. This action was very fair and advantageous to the population of San Francisco and of all California. He was also instrumental in bringing first the pony express and later, the railway line to California. He was a confidant of three Presidents.

He married the beautiful young Maria Guirado but they had no children. Alas, she was killed in a burning train accident and her body was never recovered. This seriously took the wind out of his sails and while he later married Rosa V. Kelly he still had no children. After he died in 1894, Downey County was called after him and now has more inhabitants than Galway City. Annaheim Township was called after his sister, Ann, who taught there.

He established the first successful bank in Los Angeles. He was also hugely instrumental in founding the University of Southern California.

The Great Famine arrived soon after the Downey's emigrated. Protestant evangelists came the ten miles from Athlone every Sunday with food and prayer books to convert the Tachmaconnell Catholics to their creed. There was food served, followed by sacred hymns and Protestant service. A sermon, Sunday school and more food followed this. They erected a Church at Church Park where the Catholic Church once stood. The evangelisation was very successful and soon they had over 130 converts attending every Sunday. However, in the years following the famine, when the potatoes started to grow again, the numbers fell and soon faded away altogether. All that remained of the efforts of the evangelists is the townland's name 'Churchpark'.

PERCY FRENCH

It was an unlikely source, place and time to find the Tuatha Dé Danann's magical, mystical, musical, poetic, artistic and nationalistic musings. But shortly after the famine, (William) Percy French was born near Elphin, the son of a Protestant landlord. He was reared and educated strictly Protestant in school, college and Trinity College University. Yet the poetry, music, jollity, sadness, and artistic soul of our ancient people were with him always. His songs captured the historical, social and cultural picture of the late nineteenth and early twentieth century beyond the scope of historians. His songs, music and poetry was, is and will be known and loved by many millions from generation to generation.

While an engineering student in Trinity College, and before he became aware of his huge talent, he wrote and sold for £5 the monologue, 'Abdul Abulbul Amir'. At this time in Roscommon and throughout Europe, there was a custom among the gentry of duelling to the death for little or no reason. It was a matter of honour for the belligerents, their county, country, family, name, race or friends. This was a skit on the duel between two Europeans, Abdul Abulbul Amir and Ivan Skavinsky Skavar, who fought long and hard over several hours, cheered on by an ever-growing multitude, until both were dead. He later added music to this monologue and he and others sang it for generations.

When working as an engineer of bog drains he met the real Irish and became fascinated by their country-type entertainment. 'The Mountains of Mourne' captured the beauty of Ireland, the innocence of country people, the loneliness of emigration and the inhumanity of London. 'Slattery's Mountain foot' was a skit on failed uprisings. 'Phil the Fluther's Ball' captured the pleasure, pain and ambience of great Irish peasant parties – he collaborated with Dr W. Houston Collision on those songs.

His understanding of human tribulations was honed when his young twenty-year-old wife died in childbirth with their baby daughter. He did not marry again.

Later, he left the public service and travelled widely, writing, composing, singing, reciting, entertaining, educating, enthusing and enabling many to recover dignity and hope lost during the famine. Many of his verses were written in the rough peasant language of the time and were all the better for that. No historian will ever be able to capture the poignancy, love, and heartbreak, or emigration facts like his poem 'An Irish Mother'. Just four lines of which will tell the story:

> Six pounds or was it siven
> He sint last quarter day,
> But 'tis lonely, lonely livin'
> Whin the childer is away.

His love songs captured the reality of the times, when dowry, land, money, home, heifers or better opportunities would help shape many a man's amorous intentions, overtures and advances. The saying, 'When hunger comes in the door, love goes out the window' now seemed to be believed by all. His songs were entertaining and funny but were of the times, the hard times.

His nationalistic poems, such as 'Galloping Hogan', show that he too had become more Irish than the Irish themselves. During his lifetime Catholicism was rapidly recovering and priests were regarded as almost totally wise in all things. His 'Father O'Callaghan', shows that he has a perfect understanding of this, which was amazing for a Protestant.

When he had a disagreement with the West Clare Railway, the druid in him was seen in all its funny, poetic, musical, sarcastic and lambasting magnificence: 'Are you right there Michael, are you right'.

His knowledge of all Ireland and its differing people showed him to be the only one to understand the situation. This was seen in his monologue 'Were You the Francis Farrelly?', covering all four provinces and their great differences in tradition, religion and outlook.

But his very best song was the sad, lonely, and lyrical, lament for a long-lost loved one, 'The Woods of Gortnamona', and was a perfect example of the Irish ability to sing for sorrow.

He was also a gifted artist. His painting of the dawn, with the arrival of the sun imminent, with its illuminating glow heralding its arrival for the awakening new day, was breathtaking. His beautiful, blooming, buzzing, noonday capture of his home place, in the bogs below Belmullet, for the bewitched, bewildered and beguiled Francis Farrelly was inspired artistry. 'Well, aren't you the divil' was the greatest complement a peasant's son of the place and time could pay. His serene, slanting, sunsets, slowly sinking into the Atlantic with the lengthening shadows gently veiling the shore line in serene, twilight tranquillity, brings to mind, of where he and we, may meet in eternity.

Fr Edward Flanagan of Boystown

Near the end of the nineteenth century Edward Flanagan was born in Ballymoe. Following his education he became a priest in America. At that time, in Roscommon, Ireland and the world, many poor children were neglected and indeed ill-treated in various ways. There were sayings such as 'children should be seen and not heard,' or, 'spare the rod and spoil the child.' This attitude gave free rein to bullies everywhere but especially among homeless children or those in institutions. Fr Flanagan took note.

Near Christmas in 1917 he borrowed money to rent a home for five young homeless boys that the court had assigned to him in

St Patrick's Parish in O'Neill, Nebraska. Just a few months later he was publishing *Father Flanagan's Boys' Home Journal*. By June 1918 he moved to a bigger house with more boys. He announced in his publications 'There are no bad boys. There is only bad environment, bad training, bad example and bad thinking. I have yet to find a single boy who wants to be bad. It costs so little to teach a child to love and so much to teach him to hate.' Many local parents volunteered to help him, as well as the Diocese and local nuns.

At that time in America there were coloured people who were treated as inferior, second-class and unworthy to mix with whites. Yet he wrote, 'I know when the idea of a boys' home grew in my mind, I never thought of anything remarkable about taking in all of the races and all of the creeds. To me, they are all God's Children. They are my brothers. They are children of God. I must protect them to the best of my ability. Rehabilitation needs greater emphases, punishment less.'

By early 1921 he getting support for his Home from Catholics in Nebraska and Iowa. By October of 1921 he had acquired Overlook Farm of 160 acres. It was ten miles west of Omaha and was equipped with a farmyard and some living accommodation. He moved all his children there. This was one of his sayings, 'When parents fail to do their job, when they allow their children to run the streets and keep bad company, when they fail to provide them with good examples in the home, then the parents and not the children are delinquent.' As well as school, the children helped to work the land and they produced most of their needs. He also had well-arranged, supervised games and music. He wrote, 'There is nothing the matter with growing boys that love, proper training and guidance will not remedy' and 'I do not believe that a child can be reformed by lock and key and bars, or that fear can ever develop a child's character.'

By October 1926 he had a local radio show with the Boys' Home Band every Monday evening. He had the Home's first election for a Government of students who changed the name of the home to Boy's Town. More of his comments were, 'Without God at the beginning there can only be confusion at the end', 'The poor, innocent, unfortunate little children belong to us and it is our problem to give them every chance to develop into good men and good women' and 'A true religious training for children is most essential if we are to expect to develop them into good men and good women-worthy citizens of our great country.'

During the 1930s Fr Flanagan became an acknowledged expert on childcare and toured the United States of America discussing his views on delinquency. He also had a weekly radio broadcast, throughout the United States and wrote many articles in various publications on the subject.

In 1938 two famous and successful motion picture producers from Hollywood asked for permission to make a moving picture of Boys' Town. Fr Flanagan agreed as he hoped it would inspire people all over the world to treat and help children as he was treating them. It took ten days to make the film and it was a total success when it was shown throughout the world. It won two Academy Awards, one for writers Dore Schary and Elanore Griffin and one for actor Spencer Tracy. Tracy graciously accepted the award and immediately gave it to Boy's Town where it remains to this day.

The film proved to be an inspiration to millions but in some places it took a long time, several years, or even a generation or two before good people responded and respected children. Alas, Roscommon and Ireland were such places. When Fr Flanagan commented on this he was told to 'mind his own business.' This was in spite of the fact that the same Fr Flanagan was the man to lead the first prayer in the first meeting of The Irish Free State.

After the end of the terrible Second World War, the American Government invited Fr Flanagan to Japan and Korea to arrange aid for war orphans in those countries. This was after he was appointed to the national panel on juvenile delinquency by Attorney General Tom Clarke. On his return from Asia, he reported to President

Harry S. Truman. The following year, 1948, he was asked to do the same for German war children. While there, he died of a heart attack on 15 May. Following international mourning and funeral Mass in Bows Town's Dowd Memorial Catholic Chapel, his body was entombed in his beloved Boy's Town. President Truman laid a wreath there on behalf of the American people.

On 14 July 1986, for the centenary of his birth in Ballymoe, Roscommon, the American postal service issued a stamp in his honour, another great one from our Roscommon!

23

THE GHOSTLY FIELDING
(LITTLE FIELD)

For thousands of years the Little Field was part of open country in Roscommon. It was part of a forest of oak, ash, hazel and elm. Wolves, foxes, deer, hares, rabbits, stoats, weasels goats, wild pigs and many other creatures ran, chased, fought, played, breed, killed, were killed, eaten, born, lived or died here. Those actions were serenaded and replicated in the air by crows, pigeons, hawks, thrush, blackbirds, tom-tits, blue-tits, coal-tits, great-tits, finches, wrens, blackbirds and many others. Occasionally men may even have passed this way on hunting expeditions and later perhaps, a pair or two of lovers may have communed here. It experienced rain, sun, storms, snow, frost and the ever-changing seasons, no two the same.

Even though finally it was just an acre in size it had a stony hillside with twenty-five rocks. Two of them were very big and one was shaped like a horseshoe with a sheltered middle suitable for the little people. Foreigners came and cut down all the oak, ash and elm. Hazel is all that they left, together with rotting tree stumps.

Near the end of the fifteenth century a man who had worked on the castle in Roscommon built a wall around it, as it was beside his house. He gathered large stones for the wall as there were plenty there. He dug round the hazels and got help from his neighbours to pull up the roots. Then he started digging to turn the sod to sow corn. His spade hit many stones and each one he dug up, he placed beside or on top of the two big rocks, helped by his family.

Year after year, every time he dug he hit more stones, as in this field there was only a half-foot of clay over the stony gravel. After several years he had completely covered the two big rocks and they were now known as closhes. Blackthorn bushes and briars grew among the stones on those closhes and then they were a perfect location for little people as well as several furry little creatures, not to mention the myriad of insects, worms, snails, beetles and frogs.

When the potato came to Roscommon the little field was planted with potatoes every year and it was fertilized with manure drawn from the farmyard. Over the years this made the field more fertile and increased the sparse clay above the gravel. It was a wonderfully useful field, producing nearly enough potatoes every year to feed a family for generations, until the famine. It was never planted with potatoes again, only kept for oats or hay. It was not suitable for grazing cattle, as it had no water supply.

My father had told me that his Great-uncle Tom was with the Fenians and after they were defeated the soldiers came looking for him. He hid in the biggest closh in the fielding but they spotted him and shot him dead on the spot. His blood ran down between the stones and when he was dead he was snow-white, as there was no blood left in his poor broken body. His father and mother rooted down as far as they could to try and get all the clay and stones that had his blood on them so as to give all of him a Christian burial. It's said by some that the ghost of Tom still haunts the fielding and that he is always white as snow, just as he was when his parents found him, so maybe they did not get to collect all his blood.

Not long after that, when the landlord got wind that the family had joined the Land League, he took the field off them altogether and gave it to John Hogan, a man from a mile away. Not only that, but he gave Hogan a right-of-way right by the front door of the previous owners, for him and his ass and cart to get to the field. My great-great-grandfather was mad with the man for taking the fielding and was muttering about murdering him, but my great-great-grandmother said, 'Leave John Hogan to me and I'll deal

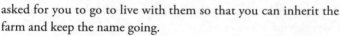

with him.' She did; she welcomed him to
the area, she gave him tea every time
he came, and she persuaded him
to join the League. After that he
told the landlord that he could
no longer afford the field and our
family got it back.'

When poor Tom was buried
there were two sons left, my
father Jim and his brother John.
My father got to rent the place
where we are now and John
married in the home place. All
but two of his children went to
America and neither of the two
married and now the brother and
sister, John and Mary, are old and have
asked for you to go to live with them so that you can inherit the
farm and keep the name going.

Then my father said, 'So you see, little man, our family has
blood, sweat, tears, hate, joy, wisdom, family lore and generations
of dreams of land lovers, buried and planted in this fielding and
you are the future of this family. And as you say that you can write,
maybe you might write down all I told you.'

I was a small boy in July 1945 when I first saw the fielding.
The two old people were making cocks of hay there. Since 1943
they had got a horse mower to mow the other fields but the fielding contained twenty-three rocks and two closhes in its single acre,
therefore it was still mowed with the scythe. The old man said his
father told him that it was always in spuds until black 1847 when
they failed, and it was in hay or oats ever since. In 1847, as usual
they had two fields of oats for the rent but lucky enough they had
a third field for themselves and this kept them alive even though
they had to sell the two cows and rely on goats until 1855.

Well, I still have the fielding and I remember where its boundaries were before I removed them by hand and tractor in the 1950s,
together with the twenty-three rocks and the closhes (and yes I did
find the (Divils) underneath and used gelignite to reduce them to
manageable size). Did I see the ghost? Not exactly, but one night
as I was lambing a ewe there I definitely felt a presence that helped
my inexperienced hands delivered live twins after a breach birth.

On half-moon nights a fleeting shadow may be noticed in the
corner of one's eye. In any case, I took a bucket-full of clay from
the inside of the horseshow rock and spread it on my grandfather's
grave. With every stone I lifted I thought of those who put them
there. Was it toil worn men or women who dug them up or did
little barefoot children carry the little ones, or were they thrown by
teenagers and were they ancestors of mine? Where are they now?
Where are their descendants? In any case they were ancestors of
some of the Irish Diaspora somewhere in the world, as no invader
would waste his time in such poor stony soil. May they all rest
in peace and may some descendants somewhere benefit from and
enjoy this information.

Ever since, the fielding has been part of a big productive field
made up from other slightly bigger fields with similar histories,
and after my time nobody will ever know it existed, where its
boundaries were or about its murder, its (Divils), or the many poor
peasants who toiled there and the many families it helped to feed
over the centuries.

Maybe St Patrick or St Bridget walked this field or converted the
ancestors of those who toiled there and who built the walls around
it in the first place. Thankfully the landlord failed to put between
neighbours. Where is he now?

24

THE SUITORS

Having reached his three score and ten years, Jimmy Brannon died, five years after his older sister Mary and one year after the 'baby' Peg. At last Maud, who had lived with her father's three old cousins since she was a child, inherited the farm in 1935. She had arrived there, aged ten, in 1920, the very year the farm was first vested in the name of Jim's ninety-year-old mother. Jim's mother and her family, like every other family in the parish, had struggled for two generations to wrest their farms from the landlord. She had gone through the Fenian Rising, the Land League, the murderous White Boys, Parnell and his scandals, the Redmond Party, Great War, the 1916 rising and endless promises and disappointments from politicians, until at last she got the farm in her name. She remembered the famine and what happened to the landless and then she owned fifty acres. It was worth the wait, well nearly; she died suddenly the next day. The excitement killed her.

Then it was left between her remaining three aging children, none of whom ever left home except Mary, who had worked in service in London for a few years when she was young. When the granny died they borrowed Maud.

Now the last of the three were dead and Maud was the owner of a fine house, stock, money and a farm free of debt and hangers-on of any description. At that time, chances like this only came in the dreams of farmer's sons who were not heir-apparent to the home farms or any farmer's sons in the area for that matter. People had to put up with living in houses with in-laws of various ages, sexes, types and entitlements. Did all hell break loose? No, all heaven broke loose with sunshine, romance, daffodils, love and happy-ever-after. That was in their dreams only.

Every single man in the parish fell in love with Maud and her farm. To add fuel to their amorous fire, Maud was a very pleas-ant, beautiful girl and a great worker to boot. As this was an area where there had been an absentee landlord there was no big house in the parish and the farms were scattered. Every farm had to have some upland, some bog, some access to water and some access to the public road. To facilitate this, the farms were fragmented and many had rights-of-way across other's land.

A few years before, Paddy Joe, a musical man from a musical family, who had been in America for ten years, came home with a bit of money when his father died and left him the farm. He bought the abandoned RIC barracks that adjoined his land and he and his former girlfriend Delia renewed their romance, married and moved in there. It was a fine two-storey, stone slated building with one huge downstairs room. It used to be the day room and that's what it was still called. They opened a little shop there, sell-ing everyday necessary items. Paddy Joe ran a dance there every Sunday night and it was a great amenity for the parish. Paddy Joe played the melodeon, little Patsy played the drums and Delia manned the door and collected sixpence each from the revellers. But then Lent came and there would be no more dances until Easter Sunday.

For the other six nights of the week, the dayroom became a ram-bling house for the men of the area. There was always a fire in the great stone fireplace and some ramblers occasionally brought bags of turf. Some played cards and some just sat around talking and smoking doogeens – clay pipes that were made in Knockcrockery, a few miles the far side of Roscommon. Even though the ceiling was high they lived in a smoky haze. Though there was a good number present all heard everything that was said. Nearly all the potential suitors were there every night. This made the topic of Maud and her farm problematic, difficult and dangerous to discuss. The first five of the seven deadly sins haunted the minds of at least some of socialisers, Pride, yes, Covetousness, yes, Lust, yes, Anger, yes and Hatred, yes – that's a lot of stuff to put in one room with a half-dozen sharp-tongued, practical jokers. Of course, all were determined to show no interest for fear of failure and ridicule. Owen, who was a pensioner, was the joker in chief: 'I don't think that Maud is much to look at,' he quietly observed. This drew sharp rebukes from three Tommys, two Bernies, as well as Tim, John and Jim. Five of the eight blushed and then everybody broke into laughter. One among them was Funny Mickey who had recently developed a huge soft lump on his neck. He laughed like everybody else.

But as he did so, some air got trapped in the lump in his neck. He had no control over this nor had he any control when the air came out again. It came out about a minute after he had sucked it in when laughing and as it did so it activated his voice box causing a long plaintive aahhh. This started everybody laughing again,

including Mickey and so the whole occurrence was repeated. In this way one good joke could keep the laughter going all night. This time it saved the bacon, or should that be the blushes, of the blushers. In future it would be different.

Because there were three Tommys, and all three had the same surname, they were known as, Toms Tommy, Bill's Tommy and Red Tommy, while the Bernies were Black and Fatty. Given the nicknames, I suppose it was just as well that none of the boys were called Willie. To make matters worse, most were related to each other. At that time, match makers tended to match men and women first of all by the valuation of their parents' farms. All farms had a valuation placed on them in the previous century for the purpose of charging annual rates. Other factors taken into account were dowry, age, looks, clergy in family, family history, and other married family members and, of course, girls in any family would only marry in order of age, oldest first and so on.

Owen eyed Joe – he had not reacted, in fact, by no reaction Owen reckoned he must have an interest or even a secret. Joe pretended not to notice Owen's penetrating stare. He seemed to have Owen fooled. A few days before the old man died, Joe had been up at Maud's farm for seed potatoes. They had filled them into sacks together in the barn. At one stage their hands touched and neither of them pulled away, they looked into each others eyes, they might have kissed but just then Jimmie arrived on the scene. They pulled away, Jimmie pretended not to notice, and decided he would ask Maud later. He didn't. He died. Joe dreamed on. What would it have been like? Could she possibly have wanted to kiss as much as he had? He got no chance to talk to her at the funeral. He would find a reason to call to the farm again.

'You're thinking of her. I know you're thinking of her,' said Owen to Joe, who awoke from his daydream, blushed and gave the game away. All eyes turned on poor Joe. He could have choked Owen. He could have choked the owners of all the leering, sneering, envious eyes. He decided to smirk and stare them down, if they were envious he must be ahead, he would definitely call to Maud tomorrow.

Tom's Tommy said he would offer to plough the cornfield for Maud tomorrow.

'Not with our horse you won't, unless I go with you,' said Bill's Tommy, 'And as you have only one horse of your own that's that.'

'We have our own team of horses,' said Fatty.

'What good is that when you are not capable of working them? You'll have to bring me to do the ploughing,' said Black Bernie.

'Who said she'll let any of you near the place?' demanded John.

'I heard she had a fellow up there last week buying spuds and that she was greatly taken with him,' said John. Joe blushed again and all laughed. He lost his cool.

'I'll have you to know that I mean to call to see Maud first thing tomorrow.'

'Aaa-hh,' said Mickey, as his air escaped. This really brought the house down and totally exposed poor Joe to sneers, leers, and jeers, and when Mickey aaaa-hhed again the whole sorry saga was repeated with many trying to keep it going for Mickey's next outburst. Joe could stick it no longer so he walked out into the night, away from the bad, bawdy bedlam, where he could have peace, privacy and his thoughts. He had a brilliant idea.

He would call to Maud's place now. She opened the door!

'Good night, Joe!'

'I, I just called ...'

'Come in, come in,' said Maud. 'My brother and his wife are still here since the funeral. This is Joe, a neighbour, this is my bother, Joe, and his wife, Mary, who were recently married and are for America next week. They're staying here in the meantime.'

'I was hoping to go to America myself,' said Joe. He did not mean to say this but he could not think of anything else and he felt he had to say something.

'Oh,' said Maud, 'and I thinking you came to see me.'

'I did, I did, I'm not really thinking of going to America but after a long time I might.'

Maud smiled, his heart jumped; it jumped into his mouth in a way that took his power of speech. It was just as well; he didn't want to put his foot in it again. He just smiled back.

Joe and Mary looked at each other. 'We're going to Boston where Mary's Uncle Peter has a job lined up for me. When we're settled maybe we'll send our address to Maud for you and you can write to us if you decide on the USA.' Maud knew her cousin well enough to know that he was fishing for information and expected a response from her so she held her peace.

'Would you like a cup of tea Joe?' she asked.

'I would, thank you Maud,' he replied.

After tea and idle chit-chat between all four, Joe went home, a happy man who had done well, or had he?

Joe had a worried night. He was all night tossing and turning and wondering. He should have said something to Maud. What must she think? He would go back first thing in the morning. He fretted so long and lost so much sleep that it was ten when he awoke. He went straight to Maud's place.

When he arrived, Black Bernie was ploughing Maud's field with Fatty driving the horses. Two of the Tommys were repairing a wall in the high field while Tim and Jim were cleaning up her bog drain, one at each end. Owen was leaning on a wall smoking his pipe and enjoying the view. When he saw Joe, he said, 'There will be sport in the dayroom tonight.' And there was – no one wanted to go to the dayroom that night but everyone had to be there to defend themselves from 'bad-mouthing bastards'.

All arrived about nightfall and talked about the weather, the new lambs, the bog, the two-headed calf in Strokestown and other trivialities. Owen could hold back no longer, 'Today I saw men ploughing, I saw others building walls, I saw others making the same drain, one at each end, but to beat of all, I saw a sleepy-headed book reader left doing nothing.' There was nervous laughter but

Funny Mickey laughed heartily. Just as the laughter died down, the
door opened and a stranger, a Yank, walked in.

'Can any of you tell me where Jimmy's Brannon's farm is?' he
said. There was stunned silence except for Funny Mickey, who
involuntary said, 'Aahhaa.'

All burst out laughing. The Yank, who was a big man, went
very red with anger but he held his peace as he was outnumbered.
When the laughter died Owen asked, 'Who's asking?' And again
Funny Mickey said 'Aahhaa.'

The laughter resumed, the Yank stormed out. Now he was not
really a Yank but at that time in rural Ireland anybody who arrived
with a strange accent was referred to as 'the Yank'. Joe followed
him out. 'Don't mind those thicks in there,' he said, 'Mickey can't
help the aahhaa; it's his swelled neck that does it.' By now all the
others had come out, as they wanted to hear more.

'Well,' said the Yank, 'is anyone going to tell me where?'

'Follow me,' said Joe, and they all did, including the Yank.

'Where is everybody going?' said the Yank.

'We're with you all the way to Maud's,' said the three Tommys,
Fatty, Black Bernie, Tim, Jim and Joe.

'That's mighty decent of you,' said the Yank.

'We wouldn't miss it for the world,' said Owen. 'It's getting
better every minute.'

They arrived and Maud opened the door, and then her mouth
in awe at the crowd.

'Who are you?' she said to the Yank.

'I am James Burke and I have come to claim the farm of my
grand-uncle, Jimmy Brannon. As I was out of the country on the
continent, I only heard of his death when I returned today and
I came immediately on the mail boat and train. The taxi man
advised me to call to where I met this crowd.'

'But neither Jimmy, nor his sisters were married,' said Maud.

'Oh yes they were, or at least one of them was. My grandmother, Mary Brannon, married my grandfather, Captain Jones

of the Connaught Rangers, in London in 1863. He was killed in a shooting accident a week after I was born. They had got married in a Protestant Church and she never told her family. When her husband died she left her baby to my father's mother and returned home to Ireland. She always kept in contact by letter and even came to my parents' wedding in Dublin in 1899. They came to Dublin to marry, especially so that she could attend. She wrote regularly to my father until he was killed in the Great War and since then she communicated occasionally with me, his only child. I was sorry when she died and I attended her funeral but I never made myself known.'

Maud was shattered, she never heard the like, neither did anyone else; it couldn't be true, but of all those present only she knew that Jimmy Brannon had made no will. 'Died intestate,' the layer said. 'With a little time and cost, it could be sorted,' he said.

Owen spoke, 'I suppose you have proof of all this Mr what-did-you-say, or what do I call you?'

'My name is James Burke, called for the late Jimmy and I have all the marriage, birth and death certificates,' he said flourishing a bundle of papers he took from a little satchel that he carried under his arm with a strap over his shoulder.

'Can I see those?' asked Owen. James handed him the papers. As Owen studied the papers, Maud and Joe looked over his shoulder. The Tommys, Bernies, Jim, Tim and John sort of sidled out the door.

'Those papers seem to be in order,' said Owen. 'But of course they will have to be examined by a lawyer.'

'They already have been,' said James, 'and I want clear possession right away.' Turning to Maud he said, 'I would be obliged if you would move out tomorrow as my wife and I propose to renovate the place and make it habitable for towns folk. We will continue to live on the mainland but we will use our farm here as a holiday home. We may employ some locals to look after the place.'

'What do you mean, move out?' asked Joe. 'Maud has being working here and running this place for the last eleven years and if you think that her neighbours and friends are going to stand idly by while you, a Jonny-come-lately, evict her, you have another thing coming.' All eyes turned to Joe. Who would have thought he had it in him? He never had a word to throw to a dog but now he spoke loud and clear with authority, assurance and a steely determination that shocked and silenced all. There must be something serious driving him.

'And who exactly are you, or by what authority do you speak? I understand that Maud came here as a destitute ten-year-old, that she was reared free for eight years and that she is working off the debt, year for year, but she has one more year to go. Being magnanimous, I am prepared to forgive the last year if she leaves tomorrow.'

'Magnanimous is it. Who do you think you are? Do you not know that we got rid of your sort years ago? From the day Maud arrived here she worked and since she was fourteen she worked ten hours, seven days a week, she has earned a much greater right to this place than you will ever have. You have a lot of big words but I will give you another one, BOYCOTT.' As he said this he opened the door and the Tommys, Bernies, Tim, Jim and John, who had been listening outside, pushed into the kitchen. There was momentary stunned silence. Envy, jealousy, enmity and rivalry were still there, but when it was a neighbour against a foreigner, especially an English foreigner, ranks were closed.

'Perhaps I have been a bit insensitive or hasty. I might be prepared to extend the time for Maud to move,' said a somewhat shaken James. Owen was bowled over by Joe and his newfound voice, vocabulary and vicious streak. Wasn't the power of love wonderful? He certainly had the measure of the Yank and he had him on the run. Could he move in for the kill? He could.

'Maud is never moving out of here, but you may be entitled to something, so if Maud is agreeable I will buy you out your claim in full, for £200. We can close the deal with the lawyer tomorrow and you and all of us will avoid a whole lot of hassle and grief.' James looked about like a rabbit caught in lamp-light, the returned stares were many and fierce. God knows what those wild Irish peasants might do. He had an offer of real money tomorrow. He would take it.

'You're on,' he said.

Joe looked at Maud, who smiled very brightly and nodded. Everyone cheered, clapped and congratulated the newly engaged couple and insisted that they seal it with a kiss. They willingly did.

The next day, James left Ireland to the Irish, and the young couple lived happily ever after.

25

WILLIE'S FIRST GIRLFRIEND

Just as his voice had become croaky, not yet fully broken, his hormones had cut in and strange things began to happen; girls had become beautiful, with shapes that he had never noticed before and bad thoughts ran riot. He had recently attended the men's mission and the preacher had warned that the Devil might bring bad thoughts to young men several times a day. This was not true for Willie. He had only bad thought a day. It started first thing when he awoke and continued all day until he went to sleep. After falling asleep the thoughts returned and were not bad or hellish at all, in fact they could be heavenly. He decided that there was nothing for it but the penance of Patrick. On the last Sunday night of July, thousands of people used to climb Croak Patrick, 'Ireland's Holy Mountain', in reparation for their sins. This was 1951.

Not many from his home place, South Roscommon, had gone the hundred miles on this mission so he was something of a pioneer. The National Bus Company ran a night bus from the nearby town with a fare of eight shillings and sixpence, and as he was only a lad he would only have to pay four shillings and threepence. After doing many, many extra tasks for his mother over the previous week she reluctantly parted with the ten-shilling note on last Saturday evening in July 1951. He cycled the three miles to catch the bus to independence, manhood and redemption at 8 p.m. He stopped to spend sixpence on ten woodbines (he could have bought his usual five for threepence, but real men flashed packets of ten) but he was still first on the bus. He sat at the very back, the middle seat of five. From here he could see the whole bus and everybody on it. He did not intend to miss anything on this, his first night out. There might be girls.

The bus filled up very quickly, starting from the front with everybody taking the next seat back. Was there something he didn't know? Then it happened, a gaggle of laughing young girls was heading down his way, seven in all. They took the four seats two forward from him and three immediately in front of him with the last girl seated alone. The last passenger on board was a sturdy lad of about sixteen. He looked awkward as he took the only remaining seat, inside the last girl. Some fellows had all the luck.

The bus took off and as it was a beautiful summer evening there was a great opportunity to see the countryside but he had eyes only for the boy and girl in the seat in front. He mightn't have bothered. She was frosty, the odd one out of the seven. She kept her back to the poor fellow and made conversation only with the girls in front and across the isle. The others hinted with their eyes that she might just look at him but to no avail. She was frigid before the word was invented. The scenery began to look attractive.

Two old couples took up the pair of seats on either side of him. They must have been forty if they were a day. Starting from the front, the bus conductor was in no hurry as he had several hours to complete the job. Thirty miles on he reached Willie. Then he had a dilemma. He wanted to look grown-up and sophisticated but it was imperative that he got half fare.

'Half,' he said under my breath as he handed the conductor two half crowns. The conductor was a kind man. He leant down and whispered in his ear, 'This is a special bus for adults only; there are no half fares, eight shillings and sixpence please. He gave him the other three and six leaving him with only one shilling on which to survive for the next twenty-four hours, so much for entertaining girls. Willie was wearing his good suit, his good shoes, no coat and no stick. He had only one shilling and nine and a half woodbines.

Everybody else had heavy clothes, raincoats stout sticks and good boots. The first half-hour on this adult bus had taught him more than several years at school.

By the time they arrived at Murrisk, the bottom of the mountain, it was midnight and many had fallen asleep. Luckily it was not raining but it was cold when they alighted from the bus. Everybody was busy putting on coats, scarves and caps and getting out torches. The shy lad he had been watching joined up with his father who was up at the front of the bus all the time. There was noise all around with lanterns hanging from stalls selling medals and pictures and there were local people shouting, 'Sticks for the Reeks!' They had stout sticks, five feet long. Their asking price was two shillings so that ruled Willie out. The seven girls approached one of the stick sellers and paid for seven sticks. He started to hand them out and then realized he had only six left. He turned back to the dark for a moment and when he looked round again he had five sticks in his hand and two sticking out from under his arm. Having pocketed the fourteen shillings he handed out the sticks one at a time until the last two from under his arm, which he handed to the last two girls quickly before disappearing into the darkness. When he turned back he had broken the last stick in two halves, making both halves useless, as they were too short. Willie had again watched and learned. How could anyone be that dishonest? What sort of parents must he have? He must have been very badly reared, where was his conscience? What sort of blackguard was he? Willie was glad that he was not like that and he never would be. He followed the crowd up to the Statue of St Patrick that was about 200 yards up and dimly lit by lanterns.

This was when he noticed that his good shoes were already showing signs of damage from the rough going and he was freezing cold. As some people were climbing barefoot he decided to do the same. He would get double salvation as well as saving his good shoes that would be absolutely necessary in his pursuit of girls in the coming months. He took them off and tied them round his neck and gingerly picked his steps among the stones, grit, gravel and muck. As he slowly progressed he got some pitiful or admiring looks from older people but from the jolly girl groups, never a glance. Even at a slow pace he got warm soon enough and he was being overtaken by most, including a few young couples who had their arms about each other, were flushed from exertion, with smiling faces and many loving looks. He wondered how this worked. They must have bad thoughts, but would they be cancelled out by the penance of the mountain? Then he saw one flushed, rosy-cheeked girl looking up longingly into the loving eyes of her boyfriend. Surely they would not break even on the sin-penance scale. Indeed, if he kept watching and thinking like this he would not break even himself. Imagine thinking like this about an old couple who were twenty-five if they were a day. Then it hit him, this was the only way that any unmarried couple could spend a night together, and even then the clergy would not be pleased as they would definitely call it an occasion of sin. Willie wished it were he.

This loving looked like the perfect thing for loving people to do yet they were told it was sinful. This conundrum occupied him for much of the way as it led down many pleasant roads. He decide that in the future he would definitely be half such a couple and if things went as he anticipated, it might be stretching it a bit to hope that the penance would be enough to redeem indiscretions. He would take his chances, if he ever got any chances.

By the time he reached the last very steep mile he was thirsty and some people were taking slugs from bottles they carried. In fact, many had bags or biscuit tins strapped or tied to their backs while others just carried bags. The stones on the last mile were very flat and if he picked his steps carefully he could always put his leading foot comfortably on a smooth stone. It was still like climbing a staircase a mile long, but he got to the top an hour before dawn. He immediately pushed his way into the little church for Mass. By this time his thirst was overwhelming and occupied all his thinking.

Just as he emerged after mass he spotted the loving couple. She was sitting on a slanting stone ridge opening the biscuit tin that he had carried up on his back. He was flashing the cash buying two cups of hot tea, at one and sixpence each, from one of the many stalls that surrounded the summit. He handed her the tea, sat down beside her and they both enjoyed it with the sandwiches from the biscuit tin. Willie sat near them but facing away, or nearly. After they were finished and the boyfriend had returned the cups, he came and sat beside her just as she produced two corked bottles of spring water from the tin. By now she was reclining on one elbow and he reclined beside her and sipped from his bottle. She left her's unopened and as he lay back with his coat under his head, she leaned in under his arm and left her head on his chest. Soon they were both asleep. Willie sneaked a look. Her water bottle was on the ground a foot from his hand. His thirst was unbearable. He checked again. They were asleep. He slowly put out his hand and took the bottle very gently. He passed it to his other hand, then slowly got up and walked to the other side of the summit. He uncorked the bottle, put it on his head and emptied it without a break. It hit the spot. In fact it hit two spots; the second one was his conscience. He had never stolen anything in his life. He never thought he would. But he just did and on St Patrick's holy mountain. That was probably much worse. He remembered the lad with the sticks, the badly reared lad, the lad with the bad parents, the lad who was just a blackguard, just like himself. While he was putting all his efforts fighting the sin of lust, the sin of theft stole up on him. He went back to confession and the priest just laughed and said it was a very small sin and not to worry about it. That was a weight off his mind.

After doing the stations round the church and Leabh Padraig (Patrick's Bed) he had a little rest sitting among the stones at the edge of the summit. He was hungry as he started down the mountain through the misty morning. It was more difficult going down without a stick, as he had to bend the knee with the weight on it as he gingerly put the other foot on a lower flat stone. Soon he had developed a method of reversing down on all fours. It was slow and laborious but the easiest way to go when lacking a stick or footwear. After half an hour he turned and sat for a rest. Just then the mist cleared, like a curtain being drawn and the magnificent Clew Bay with its hundreds of islands appeared far below. Had he died and gone to heaven? This was the most beautiful scene that anyone ever saw, with shimmering blues, greens, silver and dark shades moving with the shadows across the whole vast sea. He stared in awe. The mist returned as quickly as it went and the vision vanished. Was it ever there, he wondered, or had he just had a vision of heaven?

Then he remembered what his grandfather had told him yesterday when he heard about the intended pilgrimage. He said an old Seanchai (Fable Teller) called Brady came to Roscommon after the famine and told him the story. There was a very small, weak, bald man from Cavan called Derdi who had a terrible temper. Every time he socialised he would take offence and hit someone a mean sucker punch. As he was only a weak little rat, his victim would retaliate and give him a good hiding, some times to within an inch of his life. His wife, Fidelma, feared for his life so she went to a wise witch for advice and help; the witch cast a triple spell on the little man. Firstly, he could never again hit a Cavan man. Secondly, he could never step outside Cavan County and, thirdly, whenever his temper raised his body would increase proportionately in size, often making him a giant.

Now, Derdi had a wonderful harp that was made by the fairy people and although he did not have a note in his head he played it beautifully because it was magic. Most people thought he stole it or won it from the Devil in a bet for his soul. It was his dearest possession. A man called O'Caralan from Boyle in County Roscommon, who had music flowing in his veins, driven by his melodious, rhythmic heart heard of the wonderful instrument and longed to have it. When he offered to buy it he got a belt on the nose by the vicious fist of Derdi. That night he returned and stole the harp, rode away and hid in the Curlew Mountains. As he was passing through Kilronan in north Roscommon, his horse jumped a tree stump, his front hoofs sank to their fetlocks in the damp ground and although horse and rider stumbled and swayed neither fell to the ground. The hole made by the hoofs soon filled with water.

Derdi went mad and continued to get madder and madder until he was a very big giant. He was so big that he could have run down to the Curlews in ten minutes, pulled the head off O'Caralan and recovered his harp. But he could not leave Cavan. Imagine his frustration! As it was a very wet winter, he picked up a mighty fistful of the soft wet Cavan clay and threw it at the far-off mountains. Because his strength and anger were so great, the missile went over the mountains, over North Sligo, over Mayo and landed in Clew Bay, forming an island there. His temper and size never abated until he had thrown a hundred missiles, forming the one hundred islands in Clew Bay. Meanwhile, the holes he had made in Cavan filled with water creating Cavan's hundred lakes. That's where Cavan's beautiful lakes and Clew Bay's beautiful islands came from. Ever after, the O'Caralans were great and famous composers, singers, harpists and harp makers.

One strange incident occurred during the temper tantrum when the giant stuck his hand in the clay, his little finger hit a stone and knocked off the nail. Derdi was so mad he didn't even notice. However, as the following missile flew over Kilronan, a little piece fell off and landed in the horse track left by the fleeing O'Caralan. That little piece contained the detached nail and the blood that was stuck to it.

After his exertions Derdi shrunk back to his normal size but then continued to shrink until he was a very wizened old man, hardly able to move. Fedelma went back to the witch and asked for an explanation. The witch said 'I gave you a cure for the problem you had but I never said it would not create another problem.

Every missal that your husband threw cost him a year's energy, so now he is over 100 years old. But I will promise you that part of his family and the family of the thief will come together again and stay together for a very long time.'

'How can this happen?' said Fidelma, 'No such thief would dare come near my husband.'

'They will not see where they are going,' said the Witch. 'Now, I will say no more.'

Whether it was fate, faith or magic, McDermott was totally unaware, as he walled in a private graveyard in Kilronan, that he was enclosing the hole containing the fingernail. Nor was he aware as he buried Turlough O'Caralan, Ireland's greatest blind harpist, that they were putting him in exactly the same place as the giant Derdi's fingernail and blood. The witch was right; parts of both families are together for a very long time.

After his daydream Willie opened his eyes and there, between the fleeting clouds, he caught another tiny glimpse of Derdi's work. He then returned to his descent and only paused when a woman said, 'Look out'. He turned around and sat on a stone and there before him was a fat old woman standing precariously beside a black hold-all. She reminded him of his mother, who was fat and fifty-five years old. This lady was fatter and older, probably sixty-five.

'Why are you standing here?' Willie asked.

'I came with the young people,' she said, 'but this steep part was too much for me so they left me with the bag and asked me to stay on the level ground below and await their return from the top. The trouble is I am not able to carry this bag down the fifty yards to the bottom of the steep bit.'

'I will carry it for you,' said Willie, 'if you hold my other hand so that I can pick my steps.' She took his hand, he took the bag and they turned into a sort of four-legged creature who could navigate down the mountain quite well. When she was satisfied that they were making progress she told him he was great to be doing the pilgrimage on his bare feet, that he must be very holy, that his mother should be proud of him, that he should be proud of himself, that he was a credit to his family, that he was an example to all young people and that she was glad she met such a kind, wonderful treasure. He could get used to that.

Eventually they got to the level ground where they could sit and rest. She could easily stay sitting here until her party returned.

'Are you hungry?' she asked Willie. 'Would you like a cup of tea and a sandwich?' She said. Willie gladly said he would. She poured him tea from a flask and handed him a banana sandwich. Bananas had only just returned to Ireland after the war and while Willie had eaten a few, he had never tasted a banana sandwich before. It was delicious, exotic if not erotic, and of course his great hunger added to the sheer pleasure. He had the best meal of his life and the nicest lady he ever met gave it to him. Now he remembered that she had struggled as she held his hand to keep their balance. She had got hot with exertion, was panting from the effort and had a glowing happy face when they reached their destination. She reminded him of the girl in the loving couple. Where did that leave him?

They thanked each other, they said their goodbyes but a bond had formed between them. The lady waited for the return of her people, Willie descended to Murrisk, slept on the grass for a few hours, went into Westport and had a shilling chocolate lunch and finally got on the bus. The young lad, whose name was John, who had been shunned by the frigid girl the night before, took his seat and then the seven girls arrived. The frigid one grabbed a seat on the other side but the good-looking blonde, with the glowing cheeks, flopped in beside John, discommoding him but alleviating the upset with a dazzling smile. Even to Willie's inexperienced eyes she meant business. John thought the same, moved in a bit and said, 'There's plenty of room. I'm John, what's your name?'

'Melissa' she smiled. She actually said it but it seemed she smiled it. Willie got excited, this could develop into something exotic, he would watch, listen and learn. John was much smarter than Willie had surmised last night. But then the girls were different, very different. As the bus pulled off they were deep in chat with the other girls acting as cheerleaders. In a little while they were holding hands and looking into each other's eyes. This was great. What would happen next? Would he kiss her? Willie wished he would. Go man go, he thought to himself. The bus rocked two and fro, the girls hinted encouragement. Willie thought the lad was slow but as he watched the excitement and exertions of the night cast a great weariness on him, his eyes closed themselves, there was babble in his dreams, then a loud cheer that brought him bolt upright and wide awake. Everyone was smiling and cheering, the pair were blushing and he had just missed the kiss. Disappointment brought back the weariness and sleep returned fitfully to him, to the couple and to the girls until finally they arrived home in South Roscommon at eight o'clock the next evening. He had left as an enthusiastic, excited boy but came home as a very hungry, tired man. He had learned that costs should be checked out before journeys, not all sins are sexual, not all temptations are sexual, and not all nice girls are young and beautiful, and that the beauty of nature in sea, sky, islands, headlands, scudding clouds, mists and mountains can be a match for any human or their thoughts. He had also learned that sometimes banana sandwiches can be better than sex, that sleep can be better than sex and that even spring water can be better than sex. Nobody could have convinced him of that yesterday. Furthermore, there may be a grain of truths in myths as they come to mind at odd times.

26

THE LITTLE GHOST

Billy rode for all he was worth, out in the middle of the coach road, as at that time the edges were not tarred. The night was very wet and dark and as he had no light on his bicycle he could only make out where the road was by the outline of the trees on either side. He had a borrowed coat but no cap, with the result that the rain was running into his eyes and he had to keep them wiped half clear with the back of his hand. There were no cars, even on this main road, in 1930, so the only danger was a stray animal or another fool like himself going blind in the opposite direction. Being a teenager he took the chance.

He had gone two miles to the house of an old quack, who had a cure for jaundice. On his way there the night was fine and clear so he did not need a coat or a light. The quack's wife gave him tea while he waited for the dispensing to be done and by then the rain was bucketing down. He borrowed the old man's heavy coat but refused the hat in case he met any girls. He now realised that he was stupid as his head was drenched and of course there was not a girl in sight and even if he met girl out on a night like this, he would not be able to see her. The only reason they had the bicycle was that Uncle Tom, an uncle of his mother, had come from America two years ago to see Ireland before he died. He stayed all summer and in payment he had bought a bicycle for Mary, Billy's mother.

Then he saw her as plain as day. She was a little fair-haired girl, about eight years old, in a sort of circle of golden light. Her hair was split in the middle and brushed down each side of her face and she was wearing a yellow cloth coat, with knee-length socks and black shoes. He was gone thirty yards past her by the time all this registered. He pulled up sharp. He held out his hand in front of his face, but he could not see it in this darkness. How could he have seen what his brain told him he had seen? And what was a child doing there at twelve o'clock at night? How could she be dry on a night like this? How could he have noticed every detail of her dress and demeanour? She was no natural girl! Then what was she, a ghost? If she was real, she needed help; he could not leave her there. On the other hand, if she was a ghost, she must want him for something. He had been terrified of ghosts when he was a child but by dint of having to pass many ghostly places, he eventually got over the fear, or had he? 'Are you going back?' he asked himself. He had to, he knew he had to. He did.

When he arrived at the spot the child was gone but there was a faint trace of the light but it faded away as he watched. He went home wondering. He told no one in case they laughed at him. It occurred to him to go back the next day to inspect the place but he didn't bother, as by morning he was satisfied that what he saw was not of this world. He thought it was over but the vision kept coming back in his dreams. Then it hit him; maybe it was because of what happened last year! Was it the woman or the half crown? He decided it must be the woman!

They had only a small farm, several miles from town and as John, his father, was fond of drink, making ends meet was always a problem for Mary, his mother. They had two cows, one calving in spring for summer milk and the other calving in harvest for winter milk. The two calves were sold in harvest when one was a year old and the other was a weanling of six months. The price of those was sacred as it went to pay the rent and rates and sometimes had to be supplemented by egg or hen money. The travelling shop called weekly and Mary sold them eggs and bought the bare necessities. Hens and geese sold on big-market Saturday bought the Christmas.

At that time some people bought a ten-stone sack of flour to make bread. However, poorer families like Billy's could not afford such luxuries. Therefore, after the two acres of oats had been threshed, ten sacks of oatmeal would be mixed with ten bags of flour, on the kitchen floor and then the twenty sacks would be stored in the dwelling house and rationed out over the year. This was where the pigs came in. Ten Bonham's (baby pigs) were purchased in springtime and fed throughout the year until they weighed over twenty-stone each by harvest. When sold, each pig financed a little more than one sack of flour. This meant that pig number ten could be killed in September, salted and stored and eaten by the family over the following nine months.

They could carry four pigs the eight miles to market on their own pony and cart and they borrowed a big horse and cart from a neighbour to bring the other five. Since he was a small boy, Billy had managed the pony while his father drove the borrowed beast. Billy's purpose at the fair was twofold. As well as the driving he had to collect the price of the pigs, all but one half crown, from his father and bring it home, together with the borrowed horse and cart. John had a drink problem that he, his wife, his neighbours, Billy and the pony were all aware of. That was why John willingly gave the money and borrowed animal to the boy to bring home. At twopence a pint he could have a good day on the half crown and the pony would bring him home safely.

Billy felt like a very big man as he travelled home with the big horse and cart and his, now settled, big man's voice together with all that came with it. As well as the little bundle of notes pined into a cloth purse in his pocket, Billy had one half crown and four halfpennies in his pocket. The halfpennies were his but the half crown was part of the price of the pigs. The horse trotted along nicely until they came to a church with a pump and water trough in the parking space for horses and traps. The horse stopped for a drink. Billy jumped down from the cart to remove the steel bit from his mouth so that the horse could drink in comfort. It was then he noticed the tent further in the parking space. There was an awning on the tent where a few children were playing beside a trickster's table. The table had lovely colours and it was almost completely covered in circles bigger than a penny. There was a v-shaped grooved piece of timber slanting down to the table and into this grove one of the children put a halfpenny. It ran down the groove and eventually came to rest inside one of the circles. 'I won,' said the child, and a tawny boy who stood inside the table handed the child his own halfpenny and another halfpenny winnings. It was explained to Billy that if the halfpenny landed in the circle money was paid out. However, if the rolled halfpenny landed on a line the tawny boy won it. The circles were very big. The child had just won. Billy tried a halfpenny. It landed on a line he lost. The next one landed in a circle, he won. He played on, winning sometimes, losing sometimes, but after a while he had nothing left, only the half crown. The boy told him that if he liked he could roll a sixpenny bit and that he would have a much better chance of winning as the coin was smaller. Billy saw the sense of this and changed the half crown for five sixpenny pieces. He thought it was very decent of the boy to suggest it. They were a travelling troupe who had rented the tent space from the priest for the week. They put on plays every night and told a few fortunes as well as giving people a chance on the coloured table. When he rolled the sixpence he won, then lost, then won again and so on. The only difference with the final outcome to the halfpenny bets was that it took twice as long to lose the five six pence pieces, but lose the five he did. Devastated, disappointed and disillusioned he decided to go on home.

Then he smelt it, a strange, disturbing and nice sort of smell. When he looked around the beautiful woman from whom the smell emanated was standing beside him, rubbing his hair with her many-ringed, dark-skinned hand. 'Did anyone ever tell you that you had the most beautiful flaxen hair and that you are the most handsome boy I've ever seen,' she said. Billy blushed, felt funny and could think of nothing to say.

'Don't be too worried about a few shillings, money comes and goes and you will never be short and the longer you live the more you'll have.' This she said after she had taken his hand and studied his palm. 'Come in for a cup of tea,' she said, holding Billy by both shoulders and ushering him in through a hanging beads door. Inside it was very dark and the children had disappeared. Then the beautiful lady was kissing him. He had never been kissed before. It was wonderful and it made him feel very manly. As they embraced, things happened very quickly and he was carried away on a blissful, out-of-body experience with greater pleasure than he ever knew existed.

He remembered sort of staggering up to the horse that was grazing by the roadside. He remembered climbing onto the cart and giving the horse free rein. He remembered being asked if he wanted to continue. He remembered saying yes, how could he stop. What had he done?

When he got home he told his mother that he had lost a half crown. She went mad first, abusing him and asking how he could be so stupid. Then she stopped and said, 'Try to remember where you lost it, did you meet anyone?'

'There were people at the church where I stopped to water the horse,' he said.

'What sort of people?'

'Just children playing at a tent and a woman.'

'What sort of woman? What sort of tent?'

'They were rolling halfpennies on a coloured table.'

'Were they trick-of-the-loops? Did you gamble the half crown?'

'No only my six halfpennies first but then the boy gave me a great chance to get my money back rolling six penny bits.'

'Were you in the tent?'

'Only for a minute,' said Billy, but his blushing gave him away.

'Don't say a word about this to anyone, not even your father, and I hope you will not be fooled again,' she said. 'But do tell the priest at confession Saturday night.'

The episode was never mentioned again but the priest gave out stink and Billy never forgot. He never gambled or courted again.

Shortly after Billy saw the ghost, his father's health failed and although he lived a few years he never worked again and Billy took over the farm work. His eight younger siblings grew up and one by one emigrated to America. They all wrote fairly regularly to his mother until she died in 1960. The letters stopped after that, as Billy could barely read or write. He farmed alone with good neighbours for company. He still had the bicycle. He never married or even had a girlfriend. When Ireland joined the EU he had a bit more money and acquired a small tractor that he used as a car at weekends for shopping and travelling to Mass. He always had good health and over the years he banked a good few thousand pounds.

By his late eighties, his very kind neighbours Jim and Mary were a great help to him, while he babysat for them occasionally. Eventually he leased his land to them. In his ninety-sixth year he slipped and broke his hip. After he had it fixed he went to a nursing home for a few weeks respite. It was coming near Christmas and the local teacher and schoolchildren called to the home, singing carols for the old people. Billy was enjoying the singing and then he looked.

'That's her,' he called out, pointing at the little girl in the middle of the twelve year olds. The singing stopped.

'That's her,' he said again, 'down to the brushed fair hair, the yellow coat, the knee-length socks and the black shoes, all that's missing is the golden light.'

The child smiled. The nurse rushed over and said, 'Don't mind the doting old man. Billy, what are you thinking of, frightening the child?'

The teacher opened her mouth but said nothing. The big girls were her pupils but the little girl was her own child that she just brought along. As she looked, she thought there was something familiar about the old man.

'Where are you from?' she asked him.

'I'm from right here in County Roscommon, not ten miles from where you stand.' He had got over the shock of seeing the child again, though he could not take his eyes off her but he did not want people to think he was senile so he did not mention the vision again.

'And were you living here eighty years ago?'

'I was, and long before that, I remember the first meeting of the Free State.'

'I have a grandmother who I'm sure would like to meet you, would it be alright if I brought her to see you tomorrow?' she asked.

'Look at me,' said Billy, 'I won't be going anywhere; she's more than welcome anytime.'

The teacher and her little daughter, Anna, shook hands with Billy and said they would call again tomorrow.

The next day they were back with the teacher's eighty-year-old granny. Billy was shocked twice, once when he saw the little vision again but more when he saw the old lady who was a dead ringer for his mother, only much more glamorous and a bit older. The teacher introduced her mother, who said, 'I think you are the man I've been looking for since I was a small child. My mother ran away from home and toured Ireland with a group of play actors when she was young. She never said why. She said she met an Apollo somewhere in Roscommon and got carried away. I was the result, but she could never find her Romeo and as a result, never married. Unfortunately, she died twenty years ago. Can you help me at all?'

'I think I can,' said a nearly overcome Billy. It had never once occurred to him that there might have been a child. Not even when the good Lord sent her in a vision, how stupid could he have been all this time ... he came back to reality. 'What year were you born?' he asked.

'1930,' she replied. He held out his arms and they embraced tearfully for a long time, a long time late.

When he explained about seeing the ghost, they worked out that it was probably the night his daughter was born. It was a ghost of the future, while everybody thinks ghosts are from the past. Why was she eight years old? So that he could recognise his great-grandchild! DNA proved everything and Billy is still living, alone no longer, as he has generations of descendants.

27

THE ENGAGEMENT RING

In the 1950s, Aunt Nancy lived in London. She had come over before the war to work, had become a nurse and through the war worked her way up to Matron. This was made possible by the fact she had attended a very good national school and had a primary certificate. She had worked through the blitz night after night, risking life and limb through danger, destruction, desolation and terrible scenes of blood, broken bodies and the terrifying screams and wails of the dying, that nobody should have to witness. She was twice decorated by the war office for bravery, leadership, efficiency and dedication. Through all of this she had acquired a beautiful BBC accent as well as a house in Tufnell Park and a little bit of snobbery as she moved in higher circles. She had been stuck on age twenty-nine for several years and her biological clock was ticking. On a seemingly casual summer holiday in Ireland she had renewed a teenage romance with Pat who had just reached two score years. Pat was a glamorous cattle jobber with a little hat on the Kildare side of his head. When he proposed she said yes but she wanted an engagement ring from Tiffanies in London. After all, she wanted to impress her London friends and show that she was getting a man of substance. This did not faze Pat as through wheeling and dealing in cattle and sheep, he had acquired great confidence, a good farm and a canny ability to access the thoughts of others, way ahead of his time. Psychologists would have envied his skills.

Pat went along with the price of a wagon-load bullocks in his pocket. On arrival in Tiffanies they were met by a dress-suited gentleman who bowed, shook both their hands and announced they were most welcome. He gave Nancy several brass rings just to get the right size. During this exercise the suited gent discreetly asked Pat what price range he was thinking about. Pat replied that he wanted a good ring with a tiara of stones.

At that time a good engagement ring could be got for £50, but Nancy meant to cut a dash before leaving the posh life.

'Would a £100 be about right?'

'Have you nothing better?'

'300?'

'Something better,' said Pat. 'Do you think we're beggars?'

'Would the 500 range be suitable?'

'I suppose,' Pat replied.

A tray of rings within that range was produced and after much fitting and discussion, Nancy made her choice.

'An excellent choice, if I may say so,' said the suited one.

At this stage, a lady arrived with coffee and biscuits on a very fancy tray. After the refreshments, the suited one handed Pat a little box containing the ring.

'Will the £500 be cash sir, or perhaps a guaranteed check?'

'Hold out your hand,' said Pat and when he did so, Pat hit it a mighty slap as if buying a cow and said, 'I'll give you £250 and not a penny more.' While every head in the shop turned their way and all stopped to watch, the suited one turned pale with pain, fright and awe. He stuttered, 'We, we, don't do discounts and why did you hit me?'

'I want to see the owner,' said Pat.

'I'll get the manager,' said the suited one, but the manager was already approaching fast.

'What seems to be the problem?' he asked.

Pat replied, 'Your man here asked me £500 for this ring and I bid him half, maybe I'll do a little better but first you'll have to alter your price.' The manager, who was very embarrassed, tried to usher Pat and Nancy into a side room but Pat would have none of it.

'We'll stay where we are,' he said. 'Or is it that you think we're not good enough for the gentry around here?' The manager stared.

'Well …?' Pat said, holding out his hand.

'Well, what?' asked the manager.

'What's your best price?' said Pat.

'400,' said the manager who was totally mesmerised. Pat saw his advantage, and surmised that this softie was no match for an Irish cattle jobber and five minutes later he had the ring for £300. Meanwhile, the other couples, mostly upper-class stuffed shirt types, looked with pity on Nancy, wondering why she had not run out of the shop in anger and shame. Who on earth would want to marry a boorish cad who would haggle over the price of an engagement ring? And what on earth were those ignorant peasants doing in an establishment such as this anyhow? Despite the apparent distain, there were many envious eyes cast at the fabulous ring, and one or two at Pat, especially by the females.

As Pat handed his little hat to the suited one, he displayed a shock of wavy black hair speckled by an experience of gray. With a flourish worthy of a nobleman, he went down on one knee and loudly asked, 'My beautiful, wonderful, darling Nancy, would you do me the great honour of marrying me?'

Nancy, who had watched the whole show in silent amusement, now replied, 'Yes, yes, yes!' and kissed Pat passionately on the lips to loud applause from all in the shop. She knew she was getting an able dealer who would be well able to keep her and their children in peace and plenty all of their lives. She also knew that the £200 saved would pay to sink a well and give her running water and a proper bathroom in her house years before the neighbours. How right she was. Both she and Pat also knew that the price of the house in Tufnell Park would easily buy the fifty-acre farm that was for sale adjoining his farm. Land in north Roscommon can be variable but their farm was on a hillside overlooking a bog from where they got their turf.

Although their children have long since flown the nest, except for the one who stayed farming with wife, children, grandchildren and great-grandchildren. Nancy and Pat are still living happily into their nineties, and she still tells the story with great gusto. I wonder if many of the other couples did as well. This is what they think of the banning of turf cutting:

No more we'll cut the turf in Gorry's lovely bog,
Now this edict came from Europe, the creators of the smog.
No foreign despot ever stopped us from providing fires of turf.
Now our autocrats have barred us, will they ever have enough?
No more we'll see sods slip from the swinging slane's bright steel,
Nor watch a shapely maiden, between the barrow shafts to wheel.
No more we'll boil the eggs in the kittle for the Tay
Nor hear the lark's sweet singing on a showery April day.
No more we'll hear the curlew wild calling on the wind,
Now the turf, the bog, the good times, must all be left behind.
No more we'll leave the baby in the horse's collar there,
Nor pause at twelve bells summons, for the bog to join in prayer.
No more sweet bog pipes nor smoke or spit upon bog coals,
Nor as it simmers up, say 'Lord have mercy on all souls.'
No more the healthy hunger that bog work can create,
Nor relish big bog dinners, without a smell of mate (Meat)
No more we'll see the stork/crane winging slow his lazy way,
Nor watch the diving snipe a bleating on an August day.
No more we'll see bog water, made sterile by the caoibh
Nor can we show our children, our tradition we must leave
No more we'll jump big bog holes from the high bank to the low,
Nor dig deep bog canals to let the brown bog water flow.

No more we'll build new kishes to traverse the big bog drains,
Nor build tents of sacks and sallies to protect us from the rains.
No more we'll see the donkey with the cleeves upon his back,
Nor walk the scented heather on the brown bog's beaten track.
No more we'll share the hearth with our children, dog, and cat,
Nor keep the clothes horse by the fire or dry anything like that.
No more we'll say the rosary before the night-time fire is raked,
Nor next morning eat the hot bread that was on the griddle baked.
No more ghost stories by the turf fire with the kettle boiling hot,
Nor your mother stirring porridge in the little skillet pot.
No more kissing lovely maidens by the turf clamp or the hay,
Nor hand holding through the heather at the closing of the day.
No more we'll see the pilibín with his crested lapwing head,
Now our turf fires all are quenched, we might as well be dead.
Now came another edict not all the bogs are banned,
Now you can cut in certain places so let us see your hand.
Now at last we'll get to work and let our skill be seen,
Now my aching back is hurting, we'll send for a machine.
No more we'll boil the eggs in the kettle for the tea,
Now we'll have them scrambled with wine and finger food you see.
No more we'll hear the curlew wild calling in the wind,
Now we have double glazing that we gladly hide behind.
No more we'll hear a mother tell her child to bring in turf,
Now in central heating comfort he'll show her how the net to surf.
No more we'll smoke the pipe it's just so bad for your health,
Now instead we'll snort a joint and display our new found wealth.
No more the horse's collar with the baby's cries and sobs,
Now the baby's in the crèche for both of us have jobs.
No more we'll see the shapely maiden with the barrow on the bog,
Now we'll see her in the gym or out on the road to jog.
Nor when twelve gives the summons we'll no longer stop to pray
Now instead we'll take our cue that this is a shopping day.
Now avoid for the flock of pilibins that are circling in the sky,
Nor don't you dare look up or they'll maybe fill your eye.

No more we'll go hand-holding nor will words of love be said,
Now we'll drink until we're langered then we'll both jump into bed.
No I don't like these modern times, they make me feel a great unease,
Nor are they aisy on an auld lad but May I just stay on here please?

POEM GLOSSARY

Caoibh – hard clumped bog plant
Kish – wattle bridge over bog drain
Griddle – flat baking iron
Pilibin – lapwing
Langered – drunk
Rosary – long night prayer
Angelus – short midday prayer
Horses collar – part of harness covered with a rug and used as a baby
    sitting-up cradle
Cleeves – large baskets.
Sally – flexible bog shrub that can be bent into a tent shape facing
    away from the wind
Aisy – easy